"How come you've never—"

Radar, intuition, whatever he wanted to call it, Leif knew exactly what she was asking. "Remarried? Because I can't imagine ever replacing her. I don't see how anyone can ever measure up. No woman wants to settle for replacement status."

"So your alternative is to keep yourself locked up in this gorgeous prison of a house."

He didn't like where this conversation was going. "I have a job. I go out every day. I'm hardly locked up here." Why did he feel so defensive?

"True, but not convincing." Marta leveled her gaze to his, and he wanted to squirm out of it. "The difference between you and me is that I've never turned my back on love. Loving comes easily for me. It always has. Isn't that the point of being on this planet? We're here to share love with each other."

He wanted to get angry for her broaching a tough topic at the drop of a hat, but instead he fought that constant urge to comfort her, to wrap her in his arms and let her know she didn't have to be alone.

* * *

HOME IN HEARTLANDIA:
Finding home where the heart is

Dear Reader,

Writing the third installment in the Home in Heartlandia series was a definite challenge. I only have myself to blame since I threw in a twist that really complicated things. See, the richest man in town, Leif Andersen, doesn't have a clue what he's getting into when he agrees to let muralist Marta Hoyas stay at his house. With Leif being a hermit, letting someone else into his life feels like a full-out invasion of privacy. If that isn't bad enough, the outsider is engaging, warm and attractive...

Did I mention she's pregnant? Marta comes to Heartlandia desperate to make a name for herself, since she's just recently broken it off with her boyfriend and needs to become independent fast.

See what I mean about a challenge?

Picture me rubbing my hands together, thinking up ways to have my characters work through their fears of loss, acceptance, trust, vulnerability, pain, heartbreak. The sweet surprise was allowing Leif and Marta to naturally learn to have fun together and begin the healing process one page at a time. But then there was one more pesky little issue left to deal with—once the mural was painted, Marta planned to return home. Would Leif be ready to fall for this mom-to-be?

I hope you enjoy book three in this series. I love to hear from readers, and I always read reviews. If you're on Facebook—friend me! If you'd like to keep up with all my news, be sure to join my newsletter located at my website.

Hugs and happy reading,

Lynne Marshall

LynneMarshall.com

Falling for
the Mom-to-Be

Lynne Marshall

HARLEQUIN®SPECIAL EDITION®

Recycling programs
for this product may
not exist in your area.

ISBN-13: 978-0-373-65894-7

Falling for the Mom-to-Be

Copyright © 2015 by Janet Maarschalk

Printed in U.S.A.

Lynne Marshall used to worry that she had a serious problem with daydreaming—then she discovered she was supposed to write those stories! A late bloomer, Lynne came to fiction writing after her children were nearly grown. Now she battles the empty nest by writing stories that always include a romance, sometimes medicine, a dose of mirth, or both, but always stories from her heart. She is a Southern California native, a dog lover, a cat admirer, a power walker and an avid reader.

Books by Lynne Marshall

Harlequin Special Edition

Her Perfect Proposal
A Doctor for Keeps
The Medic's Homecoming
Courting His Favorite Nurse

Harlequin Medical Romance

Her Baby's Secret Father
Her L.A. Knight
In His Angel's Arms
Single Dad, Nurse Bride
Pregnant Nurse, New-Found Family
Assignment: Baby
Temporary Doctor, Surprise Father
The Boss and Nurse Albright
The Heart Doctor and the Baby
The Christmas Baby Bump

Visit the Author Profile page at Harlequin.com for more titles.

This book is dedicated
to the Harlequin Special Edition readers.
Thank you for giving a new SE author a chance.
I've poured my heart and soul into the Home
in Heartlandia series and loved writing the
Whispering Oaks duo before that. I have felt so
fortunate to be a part of this wonderful Harlequin
line over the past five books, and through
Harlequin Special Edition to be introduced
to loyal readers like you.

Chapter One

The last place Leif Andersen wanted to be was the Portland airport. An avowed loner, he didn't look forward to sharing his home—his sanctuary—with a stranger. But that was what he got for owning the biggest and emptiest house in Heartlandia, and it was the imposition he'd accepted on behalf of the town mural.

The absolute last thing he expected to find was this woman sporting a female version of a bolero hat, black gaucho boots and a sunset-colored wrap waiting beside the baggage claim. That had to be her—who else could it be? In all honesty, what should he have expected from an artist from Sedona? She was probably dripping with turquoise underneath that poncho, too.

Attitude adjustment, buddy. This is for the greater good. You volunteered.

Approaching the conspicuous woman, he called out, "Marta Hoyas?"

She turned her head and nodded demurely. All business, or plain old standoffish—he couldn't tell from here. Maybe she thought he was a chauffeur, but he worried about a long and awkward ride home in either case.

He approached and, seeing her more closely, was taken aback by her appearance. The term striking came to mind. He offered his hand. "I'm Leif Andersen." She'd already been notified by Elke Norling that she'd be staying at his home for the duration of her mural painting.

Marta had olive skin with black walnut eyes, the color of his favorite wood for woodworking projects. They tilted upward above her cheekbones, accented by black feathery arched brows. A straight, pointy-tipped nose led to her mauve-colored lips. *Nice.* Rather than smile she made a tense, tight line, jutting out a strong chin. Her raven hair was pulled back under the hat brim in a low ponytail that hung halfway down her back. She'd qualify for beautiful if she didn't look so damn stiff.

"Good to meet you." Marta said the words, but combined with her weak handshake, Leif had a hard time believing them. However, years in construction had left him unaware of his own power. Maybe he'd crunched her fingers too hard.

"Just point out your bags and I'll get them for you," he said, focusing back on the task at hand and not the unsettling woman to his right. Again, she nodded. Hmm, not much for conversation, and truth was, that suited him ·just fine. He wasn't looking for a friend or female company. Having lived alone for the past three years in his five-bedroom, three-thousand-plus square foot home that he'd built, well, having another person around was going to take major adjustment. So far, she seemed as much of a recluse as him, and she'd probably get lost in that great big house just like he did. They'd probably never even run into each other. Good.

She pointed at a large purple—why wasn't he surprised?—suitcase rounding the corner on the carousel and he pulled it off. Then another. And another. Had she moved her entire wardrobe?

"Let's take these to the curb, then you can wait while I bring the car around. Sound like a plan?"

"Fine. Thanks."

He rolled two suitcases. She rolled the third, plus her carry-on bag to the curb. Then he strode off, vowing not to feel compelled to get this one to talk. She wasn't here to talk. She'd come to Heartlandia to paint a magnificent mural on the city college walls, one that would depict the city's history and live up to the beauty of her great-great-grandfather's beloved town monument.

Making the trek to his car, he decided Marta wasn't exactly standoffish. He'd only just met her and shouldn't make a snap judgment. She was definitely distant and quiet, but something in the way she carried herself portrayed pride. Maybe taking a mural-painting job for a small town was a step down for her?

He'd studied her website when the college had made their final decision. She had a solid reputation and did art shows across the country but mostly in her home state of Arizona. Some of her work hung in modern-art museums and at US universities. The kind of painting she did, as best as he could describe it, and he definitely wasn't an expert, was Postimpressionism. She liked large canvases and big subjects. The style seemed well suited for their historical mural needs.

In a world of pop and abstract art, he appreciated her use of vivid colors and real-life subject matter. Hers were paintings where he knew what he was looking at without having to turn his head this way and that, squint to figure it out and then make a guess. What he liked most was her use of intense colors to make her point. In that way she was bold and unrestrained, unlike the quiet woman beneath the bold and unrestrained clothing he'd just met. Bottom line, this style would stand out on a wall at their local college, and that was all that was important.

As he drove toward the curb to pick her up, it occurred to him that beneath her cool exterior, deep under the surface, maybe all was not right in Marta Hoyas's world. This was one of the traits he'd developed since he'd lost everything he loved—an uncanny ability to read people, especially in the pain and suffering department. He could spot sad people anywhere. Saw the same look on his own face every day when he shaved. Yep, he'd go easy on the woman, and maybe they'd work out a compromise for living under the same roof for God only knew how long it would take her to paint that mural. This, too, he would survive.

He stopped at the passenger pickup curb. She got in while he put all three bags in the bed of his covered pickup truck. Being in construction since he was eighteen—he still couldn't believe it had been twenty-four years since he'd joined his father's business—there was just no point in driving a nice car.

"You ever been to Oregon?" he asked once he got back into the cab.

"Not in many years."

"Ever see your great-great-grandfather's monument?"

At last, a little sparkle of life in her dark eyes. "Yes. When I was fifteen. Beautiful."

She removed her hat, and he was struck again by her beauty. An uneasy feeling, one he hadn't experienced in years, demanded his attention, and it rattled him.

You're a man, damn it. You've always loved women. Quit thinking like a priest.

Too bad he was hell-bent on living with a dead heart. Didn't matter what this woman did to his pulse. Losing Ellen to cancer had left him devastated. The thought of ever again going through anything close to that—loving someone with all of his heart and soul and losing them— had shut him down. *Never again.*

So how the hell could he explain the humming feeling under his ribs and down to his fingertips when he looked into her dark and mysterious gaze? She crossed one booted leg over the other and stretched forward to adjust the seat belt, jutting out her chest in the process.

"Can I help you with that?" he asked, trying his damnedest not to notice her breasts.

"I've got it. Thanks."

He focused back on driving, vowing to only look straight ahead from that moment on.

Typical of Oregon weather in late September, it drizzled as he exited the Portland airport and headed toward the freeway. Being three o'clock, it would be after five before they got back to Heartlandia this Saturday afternoon. And because she had yet to utter more than ten words, and he didn't exactly feel like playing twenty questions, Leif gripped the steering wheel a little tighter and hunkered down for what he'd expected since first laying eyes on her—an extralong drive home, punctuated by awkward and strained silence. *Like right now.*

He swallowed. Fine with him.

Marta stared out the window, struck by how green everything was. What should she expect from a place that got more than forty inches of rain a year? Compared to her red-rock desert home, anyplace would look green. She glanced at Leif's profile. If he ground his molars any tighter, he'd break through his jaw. His weathered fair complexion, darkened by his outdoor work—she'd been told his was the construction company that had built Heartlandia City College—made him look in his midforties...like Lawrence. She shook her head, trying to ward off any more thoughts about her benefactor, and wasn't that all he'd wound up being? Her ex-benefactor... and ex-lover.

For five years she'd given up everything for him. Five years she'd traveled with him, met the people he thought she should meet for her career. Respected his boundaries and accepted his terms. Evidently Marta was only worthy of being his significant other. It had suited their relationship well for the first year. Hell, she'd even set up the rules. She'd rebelled against her parents' traditional marriage. Pooh-poohed her father's favorite saying: "A love like ours only comes once in a lifetime." Heck, she'd been through half a dozen boyfriends by the time she was twenty-two, and not a single one had been interested in anything beyond the here and now. That kind of love was passé. She hid behind her rebellious facade, the edgy artist, and tried to believe it didn't matter that no man had come close to loving her the way her father loved her mother. But they were so old-fashioned. Old school. She was a modern woman.

It had worked well with Lawrence at first, what with her traveling and long hours in her art studio—the studio he'd financed and built for her. But surprise, surprise, she'd fallen for him anyway, and celebrating her thirtieth birthday had made her long for something permanent. Something that said he held her above all others, that she wasn't replaceable. For three more years she'd settled for focusing on her art and waiting, but then her mother died and put a whole new perspective on love, one Lawrence could never measure up to. By then their relationship seemed more like a habit than a love affair. Even now with her leaving him, he hadn't protested...much.

Think it over, my dear, he'd said. *Nothing needs to change.*

Wrong! Everything had changed eight weeks ago, and if he thought she'd hang around forever waiting for him to propose marriage, he'd been terribly mistaken.

She attributed her change of heart to losing her mother so suddenly last year. They'd been estranged over Marta's chosen lifestyle when an aortic aneurysm had suddenly taken her life. She'd never even gotten to say goodbye. Losing her mother had cut to the core, and she'd been determined ever since to honor her mother's memory with Lawrence. He, however, wasn't on the same page— that was the phrase he'd used when she'd first brought up the subject.

Even now, with the new situation and her world turned upside down, he hadn't budged in offering marriage.

She glanced at Leif again. Dark blond hair cut short, the kind that stuck up any which way it wanted, not the carefully styled spikes of younger men. His crystal-blue eyes had nearly drilled a hole through her head when he'd introduced himself. The guy was intense and focused on one thing—getting her where she needed to be for the next couple of months. That was fine with her. She needed this break, and the job had popped up at an opportune time. She needed the money. Granted, she'd been quite sure she had an edge in the final decision, being the great-great-granddaughter of Edgardo Hoyas, the Heartlandia town monument artist. This job would allow her to get away from home and her problems and regroup, to put a little money in her bank account so she could focus on the only thing important to her right now, the…

"You okay with staying at my house?" Leif broke into her thoughts.

She'd been told she would have her own wing in a large and beautiful home.

"Oh, yes, um, that should be fine. Thank you for offering."

"Normally my guesthouse in the back is available, but I'm remodeling a house and the homeowners needed to store some things, and well, the woman had been renting the cottage from me for a couple of months—"

"I understand." She cut him off, not needing to hear another word of his long and rambling explanation.

He glanced at her, then quickly returned his gaze to the highway. "I work long hours, so I won't be around to bother you. And I keep to myself. So—"

More explanations. "We'll work things out." She should give the guy a break, since she could feel the sliceable tension in the cab.

She smiled, then noticed his poor excuse for a smile in return, but at least it softened his eyes. It also made a huge difference in his appearance. His wasn't a bad face. Not by far. He had a ruggedness that appealed to her artistic instincts. The kind of face she'd like to paint, especially when he grew older. Craggy with character. That was what it was—he had character. She suspected that something besides working outdoors had stamped those premature lines in place. Being near him made her wonder—*how would I depict this man on canvas?*

The thought struck her. Even though Lawrence was profoundly handsome, she'd never desired to paint him. Photography was how she dealt with his classical good looks. The man belonged in pictures, not paintings, a subtle difference to most, but a deep divide in her right-dominant brain.

Why did Leif live in a huge house by himself? He didn't wear a wedding ring. Was he yet another man unable to commit? But why the big house, then? A man wouldn't build a big house without the intention of filling it with family, would he?

Quiet, brain. She'd been up since the crack of dawn to meet her driver to Flagstaff to catch her flight, then, because it seemed impossible to get a nonstop flight anywhere anymore, she'd spent more than six hours, including the layover, making her way to Portland. This highway was long and tedious, except for the lovely green pines. Her eyes grew heavy and she rested her head against the cool windowpane. She'd been far more tired than usual these past two months. Whirling emotions could do that to a person. And other things…

The silence in the truck and the vibration of the road soothed her, and soon she drifted off to sleep.

Leif pulled into his driveway and around the side of his house to the circular portion where he parked. Marta had slept contentedly for the past hour, which was fine with him. It gave him the opportunity to look at her without being obvious. She was hands-down beautiful, but even in sleep she tensed her brows. What was bothering her? Having to live with him? She'd said it wasn't a problem, and these days most thirty-four-year-old women, especially an independent artist like her, would be fine with that. He tilted his head, his hunch about all not being right with her world growing stronger by the moment.

Stopping the car woke her up, which was just as well because any second now his dogs would come barreling around the corner making a happy racket.

"We're here."

She stretched and shook her head to knock out the sleep. "Oh, thanks. Wow. This is lovely," she said, glancing across the yard toward the house.

He opened his door and jumped outside, and just as expected, Chip and Dale, one blond and one black, came running full out to the fence, barking as if they'd seen a wild turkey. "Hi, guys. Hush now." They didn't listen, just kept tossing those loud Labrador barks into the wind.

Marta crawled out of the cab, squinted and smiled. Good. She was okay with dogs. Because chances were they'd eventually break into her room and lick the living daylights out of her. Though he planned to keep them out of her studio. What a mess that would be.

He pulled her baggage from the back and they made their way up to the back door. Entering through the kitchen, he asked, "Are you hungry or thirsty? I can make you a sandwich or something to hold you over until dinner, if you'd like."

"Water would be great, thanks." She held her hat in her hand, and because the house was warm, she took off her poncho and folded it over her arm. Form-fitting black, straight-legged slacks hugged her curves with a simple white blouse tucked into the waistline. He'd been wrong—there wasn't a turquoise bobble in sight. As he filled a glass with filtered tap water, she pulled the clasp from her hair and down came thick black hair curtaining her shoulders. He looked away and swallowed quietly.

"Here you go," he said, handing her the water. "I'll take these bags upstairs to your suite." The sight of her standing in his kitchen made him need to put some distance between them.

Marta drank the water heartily and looked around. The kitchen was big enough for a staff of four. The huge granite-covered center island had a second sink in it, plus a food warmer and an enclosed temperature-controlled wine rack. Lawrence was rich and she was used to the finer things in life, but seeing this *Architectural Digest*–style kitchen in a contractor's house surprised her.

She walked through a marbled entryway and into a grand room, again meticulously decorated, with a magnificent stairway and beautifully crafted, ornately carved dark walnut newel posts and railings. He'd made the wise decision to leave the matching hardwood steps uncovered, and the wood shone in what was left of the daylight radiating from the huge midceiling domed skylight.

Figuring she'd be sleeping upstairs, she took the steps and, once at the top, glanced around the wide and long upper-floor landing with accent tables and chairs, vases and paintings carefully chosen, not haphazardly picked from a decorator's warehouse. Over the balcony a huge living room was tastefully furnished in relaxing sage and

beige with pops of deep red and purple here and there.
Wow. Impressive.

"I'm over here."

She heard Leif's voice coming from her left and followed it to the French doors filled with thick etched
milky glass. Quality surrounded her.

"Here's your room."

He swung the doors open to reveal a huge bedroom
complete with a fireplace in the corner with a chaise
lounge in front of it, long sliding doors to an outside deck
and several windows.

"But this is obviously the master bedroom. I don't
want to kick you out of your own room."

"I sleep down there." He pointed to the opposite end
of the landing, to a single closed door. "Haven't slept in
this bedroom in three years." He walked across the thick
wool area rug to another set of French doors and opened
them. "Besides, this can serve as your studio while you're
here. What do you think?"

It was an amazingly big studio with a high ceiling
and three skylights, along with several other arched windows. It brought in as much light as the Oregon weather
allowed in early fall.

"This space was used for quilting, reupholstering and
furniture repair. You name it."

Was?

Even with two long workstations and a sink area,
there would still be plenty of room to sprawl out. The
space was perfect for her planning and mapping out of
the mural.

"It's phenomenal—better than my studio at home.
I love it." She stared at him, searching for a reason for

him to be so generous to a complete stranger. "Are you serious about this wing sitting empty?"

"Yes. I don't even use three of the bedrooms. I probably should have sold and moved a couple of years ago, but I built this house, and it's a part of me. I couldn't bring myself to leave it behind." He stood, knuckles on hips the way men sometimes do. Masculine as hell. Thoughtful, too. "You probably think I'm crazy living in this big place all by myself."

"I don't judge." Who was she to comment on his choice of living? "I'm sure you have your reasons."

His almost white brows lifted and his chin came up, as if he had something further to say, but he didn't make a peep. Okay, so he had his reasons, and he wouldn't be sharing them with her today. Besides, if she pried into his life, he might want to pry into hers, and that was definitely off-limits for now. She was damned if she'd share her latest news with him. They were strangers living in the same house for a time. End of story.

Besides, he'd find out soon enough.

He studied her as she checked out the studio, but from the corner of her eye she noticed him, too. He looked to be around six feet tall, lean yet solid, the kind of body a man earned from hard labor. His hand had felt rough when she'd shaken it earlier, and the naturally cut muscles lining his forearm and bulging beneath his sleeves hadn't gone unnoticed. There was a term for a guy like him—a man's man. The kind many women went crazy for.

Not her. She had other things to concentrate on for the next several months, and men had been kicked to the bottom of the list.

"Well, I'll get out of your way so you can unpack if

you want. The dresser is empty, and there's a walk-in closet." He turned to leave, then swung around again. "I'm starving, so I'll be cooking dinner. If you'd like to join me later, I'll give you a holler."

She wasn't hungry, but she knew she needed to eat. "That would be nice. Thank you."

With that, he left her standing in the center of a bedroom big enough for a princess, wondering what had happened in his life three years ago and assuming it had something to do with a woman. Didn't it always with a man like that?

Probably a broken heart.

That was something Marta could definitely relate to.

Leif caught himself humming while he cooked dinner and sipped wine. Cooking was one of the few things that brought him contentment. Well, that, his dogs and building houses, oh, and his favorite pastime, woodworking. See, his life wasn't nearly as empty as he'd thought. Building was the one endeavor that he felt came anywhere near to being *creative* in Marta's sense. He wouldn't dare call his woodwork artistic, but he liked what he saw whenever he finished his mantels and built-in bookcase projects. He'd done all of the woodwork for his home, right down to the posts, and was proud of it. Ellen had loved his special touches throughout the house, and her being an interior designer, he'd loved hers, too. He hadn't changed a thing since she'd died.

He took another sip of wine, then used clean hands to mash together the fine bread crumbs, parsley, minced fresh garlic and ground chicken with egg. He formed it into small meatballs and put them into the frying pan lined with olive oil. Not knowing what Marta's eating habits were, he'd taken the safe route and used chicken instead of ground beef for the meatballs.

He couldn't get Ellen out of his mind, maybe because of the new woman in the house. A dozen years ago, when he'd worked for his father and was still a bachelor, he'd make excuses to go back into the model homes they'd completed, knowing Ellen would be there. Her job was to stage the homes before the open-house events. He loved her style, and, more important, he liked the way he felt whenever he was around her. The first time she'd smiled at him, well, his world had changed forever.

He washed his hands, tossed the diced mushrooms into another pan, began to sauté them and took another sip of wine.

He'd taken a shower and thrown on fresh clothes after taking the dogs for their long afternoon walk through the hills. He'd put on his broken-in nicer pair of jeans instead of one of the dozens of work-worn pairs in his drawers. In lieu of a sloppy sweatshirt, his usual go-to, he'd chosen a polo shirt, one without any visible holes in it.

And he'd said he wasn't going to let having a woman in his house change how he lived. Right.

The dogs had been fed, but they still sat expectantly behind him praying for fallout, no doubt. He added the sliced zucchini and diced sweet red bell pepper to the simmering mushrooms, threw in some salt and stirred. The water had started to boil in the third pot, and after he moved the meatballs around to brown on another side, he put the angel-hair pasta in the boiling water. And took another sip of wine as he hummed another nameless song.

Moments like these were the only remaining shadows of joy he once knew. Feeling good, he tossed each dog a cooked chicken meatball after blowing on it to cool.

The table had been set and the pasta was about ready. He'd told Marta he'd holler when dinner was served, but somehow that didn't seem right. He'd given her plenty of time to unpack and get organized, so he turned everything down to simmer, quickly covered the distance from the kitchen to the stairway and took the steps two at a time to tap on her door. The dogs followed and beat him there. Just as he was about to knock, he saw her shadow behind the thick milky glass and the door swung open.

"Oh," she said.

"It's time for dinner." The dogs watched her curiously. So did he.

She'd changed clothes. Had put on lounging-type pants and a bright green patterned tunic over a black tank top, which dipped low enough to display cleavage.

"Thanks," she said. "I could smell the cooking up here."

As they descended the stairs he said over his shoulder, "I hope you're hungry." He got a murmured response.

They entered the kitchen. She held back a little bit, but he pretended he didn't notice.

"I'm having wine. It's a blend of three whites and is pretty good. Would you like a glass?"

"Oh, no, thank you. Water will be fine. Actually, make that milk if you could."

Okay, so she wasn't a drinker. No problem. "Kent, my doctor, has me on fat-free milk. Is that okay?"

"Yes. Fine. Thanks. May I help with anything?"

"You can take the plates to the table while I get your drink. How much pasta?"

He used a pasta spoon to measure the cooked angel hair for her plate.

"A little less, please."

They made eye contact so she could direct him on the portions for the sautéed veggies and meatballs. Either this one was a small eater, or she didn't care for what he'd prepared. Either way, he wasn't going to let it bother him. Then he served his own plate with generous portions and handed that to Marta, as well. She carried them to the table as an idea popped into his head. He'd wired the entire house for sound and rarely used it anymore. So he flicked a switch, and they had music to dine by. But then he quickly worried she'd get the wrong impression—like this was a date or something.

"Is music okay, or do you prefer silence?"

She listened to the light classical sounds and nodded. "It's fine."

He poured her milk, topped off his glass of wine and brought them both to the table. The basket of whole-grain sourdough bread was already in place. So was the butter. It had felt dumb for them to sit one at each end of the long dining table, and he thought it would be too casual to sit at the breakfast bar for their first dinner together, so he'd sat her to his left, like he and Ellen used to do.

They ate for a few minutes with the soft music in the background but without conversation. After a bite of the chicken meatballs, she complimented him on his cooking. She seemed to mostly move her food around the plate, eating very little. She did drink her milk and managed half a piece of bread, though.

He enjoyed his meal and decided not to worry about this grown woman. She could and would take care of herself. Maybe she was nervous about this new project. Or, even though she'd said she didn't have a problem staying here with him, maybe she was uncomfortable about the living arrangements. He could make guesses all night.

"You're a good cook," she said again. "I wish I could eat more, but my stomach has been giving me fits lately."

She did look a little drawn, but because of her olive complexion it was hard for him to tell if she was paler than usual.

"Sorry to hear that. I've got antacids if you need—"

"No. No. I'll be fine. Thanks."

There she went again cutting him off. His impression so far was she only tolerated being around him. He'd make a point to stay out of her way from now on.

But a meal was meant to be accompanied by conversation, and damn it, he couldn't enjoy this delicious dinner—if he did say so himself—nearly as much in silence. Leif racked his brain for an ember to spark a conversation.

"So tell me about your work. Your studio. Your home in Sedona."

She took a small bite of zucchini, then smiled. A genuine smile, and it almost pushed the wind out of his lungs. "Are you familiar with my work?"

"I've been to your website. You're very talented. Obviously."

"I've lived in Sedona for the past eight years, though I grew up in Phoenix. My father is still there. I was fortunate enough to acquire a benefactor who believed in my painting. Without him, I don't know...well, I doubt I'd be nearly as successful." She took a sip of milk.

"You seem to like to do landscapes. Do you paint outdoors?"

"Sometimes, but it gets terribly hot in Sedona several months of the year, so mostly I spend a few days taking photographs of what I want to paint at different times of day. I try to capture the perfect lighting, then I blow them up, cover my studio walls with the pictures and go from there."

He thought of a few more questions to prod her along, but his mouth was full so he waited.

"I have an art showroom downstairs and I live upstairs where my studio is. I'm fortunate to have a small staff working for me so I can concentrate on painting."

"You're not married." It sounded matter-of-fact, and maybe intrusive of her privacy, but he'd had a glass and a half of wine and just sort of blurted it.

"No." She looked at her plate, but just before she did, the subtle crinkle of her brow made him wonder if he'd hit a sensitive nerve.

She was what, thirty-four? Did women these days still get touchy about being single after a certain age? What did he know? He'd lived in a cave for the past several years. At forty-two, he'd often felt his life was over in that department. Now, that was one hell of a pill to swallow for a perfectly healthy man, but, nevertheless, that was how he felt. He took another sip of wine; the glass was almost empty. He could save this sorry excuse for a conversation. He used to be good at it. *Think back, Leif. Or, here's an idea—pretend she's a man.*

"Well, I've got to tell you," he said. "I think your painting will be perfect for the mural."

"Thank you." She still looked at her plate, moved some pasta back and forth.

"So walk me through this mural-painting process. I'm a novice."

She popped a small piece of bread into her mouth and drank a sip of milk. Then she said, "I have to be honest and tell you I've never painted an entire mural before."

Now, that was a surprise. Maybe that was what she

was nervous about. Come to think of it, he'd only seen her huge canvas paintings at her website. She'd also submitted a preliminary mural design, which had helped the committee make their choice.

"But I've put a lot of thought into this project, and I've studied how it's done. First, I lay my idea out on a grid. Since this is the biggest painting I've ever tackled, I'll go about the process one step at a time. I've already started the grid and plan to paint it in the one inch to one foot scale first. After that I'll transfer it to the wall one section at a time."

So that was why she had three suitcases. One was probably filled with supplies.

"Will I need to prepare the walls for you?"

"Oh, good question. Yes, please."

"Just tell me what you need and when and I'll get her done."

"Great, thank you. That won't be for a while, though."

They continued chatting about the steps to undertaking this project, both engaged and distracted from whatever other cares they had. He promised to take her to the college to see the outdoor walls soon. After she explained what needed to be done, he planned to remove the stucco and prep the walls to her specifications while she painted her smaller-scale grid.

After dinner she helped him wash the dishes, then she went on and on about how beautiful his house was and how extraordinary her living quarters were. Suddenly the day, and meal that had gotten off to a rocky start, was ending on a much better note.

Because she'd eaten so little, he showed her where the leftovers would be and several other choices for snacks, making sure she understood the *mi casa es su casa* philosophy they needed to agree on. It was called Scandinavian hospitality or the Viking code and the god Odin had originally laid down the law in the poem *Havamal*: "Fire, food and clothes, welcoming speech, should he find who comes to the feast."

She thanked him again and said good-night, then quietly went up the stairs. He planned to take the dogs out for one last quick walk, but before he did, he watched her hair sway as she ascended the stairs and, to his surprise, he also noticed the twitch of her hips. But what man wouldn't?

Having a woman in the house had already changed things. A life force was again coming from that end of the second floor. The often overbearing emptiness of the house seemed tamped back a bit, and it felt...well, it felt damn good.

Later, when he laid his head on the pillow, he tried to remember the last time he'd engaged a woman in a conversation for more than two minutes. Not counting women trying to engage him in conversation, like his guesthouse renter, Lilly, who was always full of questions about the town. But what could he expect from a reporter? Or little old ladies at the market with single daughters or granddaughters.

Nope, he'd initiated this conversation tonight, and somehow he'd managed to draw Marta Hoyas out of her shell, even if only for a little while. The thought made him happy, a foreign feeling for him. Well, he'd had a couple of glasses of wine, which probably helped that along.

Yeah, that had to be the reason for that goofy-feeling grin pasted on his face.

Not the beautiful woman from Sedona.

Chapter Two

"Ellen?" Leif rolled over in bed, mostly asleep. "Ellen?" No flash of a dream came back to him like usual. What had driven him out of deep sleep thinking of his dead wife? And what time was it? He looked at the bedside clock—quarter to five. Almost time to get up anyway.

Leif sat up, gave a quick shake of his head and pulled on his jeans for the short walk to the hall bathroom. Another inconvenience of having a woman in the house. As he woke he understood he must have been dreaming about Ellen, but usually when he did he remembered it. He didn't remember anything about this dream. If that was what it was.

He heard a sound and stopped. It was very faint but undeniably a sound he remembered.

He stood quiet and listened harder. There it was again. Retching.

The old and familiar heaving from when Ellen had suffered through chemotherapy came rushing back. He must have heard that unmistakable sound in his sleep.

Retching? What was up?

He squinted and listened. It had gone quiet again, but the puking sound had come from Marta's room. Had she gotten food poisoning from what little she'd eaten last night? Damn, that would be horrible. He felt fine, so why would she get sick?

After he finished his quick pit stop and washed his hands he heard more retching and fought off a wave of terrible memories. *Oh, God, Ellen, what you went through*. He strode to the end of the hall, not wanting to be nosy but unable to let this lie. It was quiet again.

Marta was curvy—not ultrathin like anorexics or bulimics tended to be. What a crazy thought to even entertain, that she might have an eating disorder. That couldn't be it. But she'd picked at her meal and looked queasy during dinner, even said her stomach had been giving her fits.

She'd also refused alcohol.

A lot of people didn't drink. But a warning thought planted inside his brain and made him back off as he heard one more round of intense dry heaves. He wanted to help her out, but it could prove embarrassing for her, and that wasn't his intent. She needed—deserved—privacy. If she was sick, he'd gladly take care of her, but not without an invitation. She was a grown woman and he assumed she wouldn't hesitate to ask for help. Unless she was one of those superproud ladies who couldn't ask for anything.

He ran his hand through his hair, torn. *Let it be, Andersen*. He listened to his intuition stemmed from the fact she'd refused any wine last night. A troubling thought of what a woman throwing up first thing in the morning usually meant made him step away from the door, then he headed back to his bathroom for a shower.

Later, Leif had eaten and was feeding the dogs, having decided to take them with him over to the job for the day. He'd promised to finish the add-on to Gunnar Norling's house in six weeks, and Gunnar had offered to help as much as possible. That meant today, before the sergeant's shift at Heartlandia PD, they'd install the triple-paned windows that had arrived yesterday. Even though he'd been driving his crew hard on this project, no way would Leif ask them to work on Sunday. The guys needed at least one day off. He and Gunnar could handle it.

After both dogs took a quick whiz, he whistled for them to jump into the bed of the truck. He'd removed the cover and had thrown in his window installation tools. Just as he finished closing the tailgate, he noticed Marta standing in the kitchen doorway in a robe that looked like a Native American blanket. With her hair parted down the middle and not brushed, it tumbled over her shoulders in a wild mess. The vision moved him in ways he hadn't felt in years. It also bothered him to react so viscerally to a near stranger. She might be pregnant, for crying out loud.

"Where are you going?" Curiosity knit her brows.

"I've got a job today. I left you a note in the kitchen. Sorry, but I didn't want to disturb you."

"Oh, okay." She folded her arms. "That's all right, then. I'll wait to talk to you later."

"Is there anything you need?" He thought back to the noises emanating from her suite earlier.

"Besides a good night's sleep and peace of mind?" She offered a wan smile. Her pained look made him want to wrap his arms around her and tell her everything would be okay, and what was up with that impulse? But other than having a pretty solid hunch, Leif didn't know what her problem was. He really didn't have a clue if things were okay in her world or not. Obviously, something had robbed her peace of mind.

"Do you want me to stick around? Take you anywhere?"

She shook her head. "No. I'll be fine. I'll work on the grid." She glanced down at her slippers, then quickly back up. "I would like to talk to you about something when you get home, though."

"If it's urgent, I'm all ears."

"Not really urgent. I'll talk to you later." She started to back away from the door.

"Okay, then." Leif opened the cab door and started to get inside.

"Oh, hey, what time will you be home?"

"Gunnar's got to be at work at three, so I'll see you before then." It felt eerie having a woman ask when he'd be coming home after all these years. "Do you want me to bring some lunch or anything?" *Saltine crackers?*

"You've got plenty of food here. Thanks. We'll talk later." With that, the beautiful, straight-out-of-bed vision disappeared from the door.

As he backed out the truck, Leif was certain Marta was going to tell him she was pregnant, and he chided himself for having already developed a little crush on her.

On a pregnant lady. How desperate is that?

Seven hours later, Leif returned home and put the dogs in the gated backyard and pool area. He went in the back door, took his dirty shoes off in the laundry room, then headed to the kitchen. The house was quiet enough to hear a drip of water in the sink. As he turned the faucet completely off, he noticed a bowl in the sink. She must have eaten cereal, so at least that was something.

He headed up the stairs in his stocking feet. Not wanting to come off as a sneaky surprise, he cleared his throat and made a fake cough, preparing to hear her news— *I'm pregnant.*

"Marta?" he said, taking a turn for the studio.

"I'm in here."

He entered the bright white room, thinking maybe he'd overdone it with three skylight panels, but Ellen had always loved it, saying it was the perfect natural lighting for intricate stitchery. Maybe Marta would like that, too.

She was hunched over a table, a long piece of white paper spread along the entire length. A second piece of paper was laid out on the other worktable.

"Come here and have a look," she said. "Tell me what you think so far." She glanced up, her hair pulled back into a low single braid, though a few wavy tendrils had broken free around her face. He fought the urge to tuck one behind her ear. She wore a teal-colored plaid flannel shirt with the sleeves rolled up and holey old jeans. He couldn't help but notice she still wore her slippers.

"You could have turned the heater on, you know," he said, worried she'd been cold all day.

"I've been fine. The skylights bring in a lot of warmth."

Good to know. He stepped closer, her dark eyes and olive skin quickly reminding him he was still a man. She used a graphite pencil and a yardstick to draw the final sections of grid over her mural sample.

"This is the tedious part," she said, then stood. "Come and look at this. Let me know what you think."

Long sections of Heartlandia history were sketched and laid out before him, beautifully depicted with her natural and flowing artistic style.

"Notice something?"

How beautiful you are?

Actually, something besides the fact she smelled like cinnamon and ginger did draw his attention. He pointed to a blank area at the beginning of the mural. "That?"

"I've been concerned about this project from the start. All the information the college provided me was exceptionally helpful, but when I began my sketches, I kept feeling blocked right here." She pointed to the beginning.

"I wound up having to work backward because this strange sense of darkness stopped me from advancing. I got the Chinook and fisherman part just fine, but something—pardon me for sounding overly dramatic, but *forbidding* is the only word I can use to describe it— tugged at me to start even before then. Yet no one sent any information about before that point."

Ah, jeez. Was this woman a psychic? Were artists more in tune with secrets?

For the past few months a private panel had been meeting at city hall to discuss this exact matter. Sleepy little Heartlandia hadn't been founded by the Scandinavian fisherman with the help of the native peoples—the Chinook—as they'd always assumed, but by a scurrilous pirate captain named Nathaniel Prince, also known as the Prince of Doom.

The perfect little tourist town had been thrown into a dither over this newly discovered fact, in no small part thanks to Leif. While breaking ground for the new college, he'd dug up an ancient trunk filled with journals. The pirate captain's journals. After authenticating the captain's accounts and having Elke Norling, the town historian, decipher them, their worst fears had proved true. There had been a concerted effort somewhere back in time by the people of Heartlandia to suppress the truth, and now it was time to come clean.

Plans were in place for a town meeting, where the information would be revealed by mayor pro tem Gerda Rask, with Elke by her side. And Lilly Matsuda, the new journalist at the *Heartlandia Herald*, had agreed to run the entire historic findings in a three-part story. But that only solved the first problem; the second was even worse. Captain Prince had alluded to a second trunk filled with gold coins and jewels…buried at the Ringmuren. Which happened to be sacred burial ground for the Chinook. Even now, the thought of dealing with this town-wide problem made his head want to explode, and because he was the guy who'd kicked off the whole mess and he'd been on the secret panel from the start, he couldn't avoid the predicament or the fallout.

The bigger question, right this moment, was how much should he tell Marta. And how crazy was it that she'd sensed a problem without knowing about Heartlandia's dark side? One thing he did know—he'd wait a bit, feel things out more, before saying a word to her.

"The problem is—" Marta watched him as she spoke. Was she trying to read his reaction? He went still, willing his face not to give anything away, afraid he already had. "The problem is Elke gave me scant information before this shipwreck where the Scandinavian fisherman first arrived in these parts. I think that's the issue. What about the native people, the Chinook? I need more information to do the mural justice."

He inhaled, not having a clue what to say or how to handle things right this instant.

"I hope you don't think I'm crazy. I assure you I'm not a woo-woo type at all. It's just this dark feeling I keep getting has clouded my vision of the project from the start. Once I'm past this initial area, I'm fine." She pointed to the beginning, the blank part of the mural, tapping her finger. "But this part right here, well, something isn't right."

"I'm sure there's a logical reason, and we'll find it while you're here." *A cop-out for sure, but the best I can do right now.*

The only thing Leif could think of at the moment was to distract her. Because he sure as hell couldn't give her a truthful answer, not before the mayor made her official announcement about this very thing to the people of Heartlandia. And not before all hell broke loose. Man, maybe he *should* give her a heads-up first.

"So is this why you've been all keyed up? Not able to eat? I think I heard you throwing up this morning." May as well come clean.

She took a quick surprised inhale, then nailed Leif with open, honest eyes. "I see I'm not the only one gifted with intuition." She smiled. "Look, since you're being direct, I will be, too. I'm pregnant. Eight weeks. Sick as a dog most mornings. Can't wait for this first trimester to pass. It's my first pregnancy, so all I can do is believe the books."

Leif had been right, but hearing the words from her mouth took his breath away and made him suddenly want a drink. He strode to the sink, opened a cupboard and found a glass, filled it with filtered water, gulped a few swallows. "Would you like some water?"

She nodded, probably more to be polite than for any other reason. He filled a second glass for her, handed it over, then engaged her eyes. He saw questions in hers, and realized this moment would speak volumes about his character.

"You want to talk about it?"

Marta took a sip of water, apparently thinking, then sighed quietly. The expression on her face seemed to communicate, *I may as well.* "I've recently broken up with a man I'd been involved with for five years." She looked resigned, not brokenhearted.

Leif was already stuck on the first sentence. Didn't people usually get together when they got pregnant, not break up? Was she waiting for this guy to show up and take her home?

"I wasn't trying to trap him or anything. The pregnancy was definitely an accident. But when I told him, I thought maybe he'd ask me to marry him." She put the glass on the counter, folded her arms, paced toward one of the windows and gazed outside. "He wasn't exactly happy with my news, but at least he didn't say he didn't want me to have it or anything." She glanced at Leif over her shoulder, then back outside. "I got the feeling he just didn't give a damn. 'Things don't have to change' was all he said." She swung around, suddenly animated, an accusing expression on her face, as if Leif was a representative for all of the lousy men in the world. "What was that supposed to mean? Of course things would change. Everything had *already* changed. We'd be parents." Out of nowhere she'd found a tiny cuticle on her index finger to bite and went for it with gusto. "I'd given him five years of my life. I'd given him everything I had. And now I'm pregnant and he isn't particularly interested in that part." She used the back of her hand to brush the air. "'Just take care of it,' he said. 'Get this pregnant part over with, then things will be back to us again.' How selfish of him. How foolish of me to think he'd ever want to marry me." Rather than say more, she curled her bottom lip inward and bit it.

At least she wasn't crying. He wouldn't know what to do if she started sobbing.

Leif had been right. He'd recognized a fellow traveler on the broken and hurting road. Turned out he wasn't the only person in this house whose spirit needed some mending.

"I'm very sorry to hear this. Uh, not that you're pregnant, but about your breakup. That things didn't work out for you."

"I understand. Thanks. I guess that's life, right?" She lifted her chin.

Yeah, he knew about "that's life." It had kicked the spirit out of him, too.

"Maybe he'll come to his senses while you're here."

"I no longer care if he does. It's over."

"What about the baby?"

"Look, I'm sorry to drag you into my problems," she said.

His first response was to say, "That's what friends are for," but they were practically strangers. "For the record, I'm glad you opened up."

She tossed a surprised glance his way. "Thank you."

He needed to do something to change the mood, to move away from the heavy subject, to keep himself from walking over and taking her into his arms for a tight, long and comforting squeeze. He hardly knew her, yet he already felt the urge to protect her.

"I've got an idea," he said, glancing at his watch. "It's only two-thirty. Why don't we get outside and take in some fresh air? I'll show you the City College and where your mural walls are located. What do you say?"

She glanced back again, as if his idea wasn't half bad.

"Who knows, maybe it will help you get unstuck."

Her face brightened at the suggestion. "You're on. Just let me change my shoes."

Marta enjoyed the distraction of driving around the quaint and colorful city of Heartlandia. She looked out the window, taking it all in.

"We're heading north past Heritage, the main street in our downtown section. That's the Heritage Hotel, oldest building in town. Now we're heading toward our hill that we like to call a mountain, Hjartalanda Peak. It's not exactly Saddle Mountain, over there—" he pointed eastward toward a large pine-covered mountain range off in the distance "—but it's good enough for us." He smiled at her, and a weird fizzy feeling flitted through her chest. Those eyes. Must be those crystal eyes.

"Heartlandia City College is halfway up the hill between the Ringmuren wall and downtown, which took a lot of campaigning to approve clear-cutting a large section of our pines. In the end we agreed that we needed the jobs, the incentive for our kids to stay home to go to college instead of leaving the area and the influx of new blood the school would bring into town. Plus, I promised not to cut down one more tree than necessary and to plant a whole lot of other trees somewhere else." He looked at her and smiled again. "I'm not going to lie—I'm very proud of the college."

"Your company built the entire college?"

He nodded. "My father started his construction company fifty years ago from scratch. He built half of the bungalows and sloping-roof Scandinavian log houses you see scattered across the hills. When he was fifty and I was twenty he developed rheumatoid arthritis and asked me to take on more responsibility for when the time came he couldn't do the hard work himself. I learned the business from the ground up for the next ten years, and when my dad moved to Arizona at sixty, I took over. I'm glad to say the business didn't fall apart when I stepped in." He flashed a smile she could only describe as charming, and there went that fizzy feeling again. "I've actually brought the company to a new level but only because of the foundation my father laid down for me. And the work ethic he instilled in me."

"That's very impressive," she said, meaning it.

"Thanks."

They pulled into a large lot and parked close to a long and low building to the left of the main three-story administration center and a cluster of other one- and two-story structures. They'd gone the clean, midcentury modern route with a definite Scandinavian influence in architecture.

He opened the door for her, and she followed him toward the long, low bungalows.

"This is the history quad," he said. "We thought this would be the best place to put your mural. See those walls over there?"

She nodded and sped up her pace to keep up with him.

"Those are your walls."

She liked the sound of that—her walls.

"The mural will be visible to everyone as they enter the campus. Pretty good, huh?"

"Fabulous. Now I'm getting excited but nervous, too."

"No need. You're very talented. I'd say quit stressing about your artist's block. Things will work out in their own way. You may be surprised. Just keep getting your grid together."

She walked ahead of him and followed the long twelve-foot-high walls, imagining what her mural would look like when she'd finished. "Wow, this is great. See, I'm getting goose bumps."

He politely took a look at the raised hair on her arms. "I'll get right to work prepping these walls for you. When you're ready to start, nothing will hold you back. I guarantee."

"I wish I had as much confidence as you do." What if she couldn't break through the mental block about the beginning of Heartlandia's history? What would she do then? She'd been hired based on two reasons, and she was sure the first carried the most clout. Her great-great-grandfather had designed and built the town monument. Also, the mural committee liked her style of painting. She'd only done extralarge canvas paintings so far and they were much smaller than these walls, but the committee had chosen her once she'd submitted her preliminary vision for these walls. They must have seen something they liked.

"Are you kidding? You're a fantastic artist. Listen, if it will help I'll arrange with the school librarian and the history department chair to get you more books and photographs from our town. We have a great Maritime Museum with loads of old pictures, but it's undergoing renovations after a recent fire. There's all kinds of stuff for you to look at right here."

"That's really nice of you. Thanks." It meant a lot to her to hear Leif praise her work.

"I want to help in any way I can. I built this college and I want to see it at its full potential. Your mural will make all the difference in the world."

If she could only believe in herself half as much as he did. She couldn't let her personal circumstances and disappointment hold her back on this project, or let the insecurity of not being wanted by the father of her child spread to her art, and she silently vowed to make this mural her best work yet. She needed the job for financial security and the recognition it would bring for her and the baby's future.

"So what will you need?"

Lost in her thoughts, she glanced at him blankly.

"For painting," he said.

"You mean paints?"

"Yeah, and brushes and drop cloths and any other supplies."

"Acrylic mural paints are a must, and I'll be needing gallons and gallons of the colors. It might be tough on the city budget."

"Do you have a list of your colors yet?"

"I have a good idea what I'll need."

"Then, let's go shopping."

"Are you serious?"

"Dead serious. It's four o'clock, so we better hurry because our hardware and paint store closes at six on Sundays."

With that they rushed back to the truck and hopped

inside. Marta hadn't felt this excited and full of energy in weeks.

"Tell me about your family," she said as they drove, deeply curious about the man, a near stranger, who had so much faith in her abilities.

"My people came here in the 1800s. They were fisherman, like most of the other Scandinavians in this area. I think my first relative might have been an indentured servant on a fishing boat from Denmark. I'm Danish, by the way. Well, I'm actually an American of Danish descent. I guess you'd say that is more accurate."

She understood. "My ancestors are from Argentina, but like you, I think of myself as American with Latino roots." Her mother had always been too traditional for her taste, and overprotective, but that was to be expected and it was her way of showing she loved Marta. But they'd argued constantly about her free-living lifestyle, and it had driven her away. Now she wished with all of her heart she could have mended their differences before her mother had died. Family had taken on a whole new meaning eight weeks ago.

Leif ran down his brief genealogy chart while they headed for the paint store, then he suddenly hit a bumpy patch in the story. "My father died eight years ago, so we moved my mother back here from Arizona where they'd retired. I'd originally built the guesthouse for both of them to come and visit whenever they wanted. Five years ago, Mom had a massive stroke and died on the way to the hospital."

"I lost my mother last year and can only imagine how tough it must be to lose both parents."

"Yeah, I guess that makes me an orphan."

"I believe you're right." So who had he built that big gorgeous house for? "Were you ever married?"

"Yes."

Of course he was a traditional kind of guy. The kind of man she'd never run into while living her sophisticated artist's life.

"I built my future wife's dream house as a wedding gift. I had to do something to get that woman to marry me." He worked at a smile, but it came off as wistful and far from his eyes. "My wife was Norwegian, since we're talking about Scandinavian ancestry."

"Are you divorced?"

"No." He grew quiet for a moment. "She died from ovarian cancer three years ago."

Things suddenly added up—why he'd offered her the master bedroom and studio, why he hadn't slept in that room for three years, why he stayed in the big house by himself rather than sell it. "I see. I'm very sorry to hear that." Not only was he an orphan, but he also was a widower and had lost everyone he loved. "That's a lot of people to lose in a very short time."

"You're telling me." He inhaled as he parked and cut the engine. "But losing my wife was the hardest thing I've ever been through in my life." He gazed solemnly out the windshield. "Ellen... She was the one who suffered the most."

The thought sent a chill through her. "You don't have children?" She turned toward him rather than move to get out of the car.

He faced her, too. "That's how we found out about her cancer. We wanted to be a family. A big family. Decided to have a bunch of kids. We tried for that first baby for a couple of years and finally decided to go the fertility clinic route, first checking out my plumbing, then hers. That's when they found her cancer. Already too late."

His distant glance over her shoulder was tinged with agony. It nearly broke her already raw heart.

Overcome with compassion and respect for this man who'd lost everything he'd loved, making her own situation pale in comparison, Marta leaned across the bucket seat, reached for his forearm and squeezed. "You suffered, too, Leif. I can only imagine."

Their eyes locked for a couple of moments. New understanding passed between them. He studied her as if he was trying to figure out if he appreciated her concern, or if he resented the pity. It wasn't pity, as far as she was concerned. This connection was an honest desire to offer him comfort. She wondered how he'd managed to survive losing his entire family. How lost he must be all by himself. In such a short time, she'd already figured out he deserved much more than this lot in life. And she had nothing to complain about. She had her health, a baby on board and a profession she loved. She almost had everything…except a man.

"If it wasn't for the business, I think I would have gone nuts."

"You're a survivor. A person can tell that about you right off." She started to remove her hand, but he reached for it and squeezed, holding tight for a moment before releasing her. His warm touch surprised her. In twenty-four hours it had already changed from their initial mechanical handshake.

"What do you say we go shopping?" He'd obviously had enough of this heavy conversation. His story was probably the last part of Heartlandia history he'd wanted to dig up today, but she was glad he had. It helped put so many things in perspective.

"Let's do it." She smiled and he returned it, in obvious relief. They'd come to a realization—they'd both been knocked in the teeth by life. The major difference was his love had died, and though she'd broken off with the person she once thought was the love of her life, she had a new life growing inside her. She wasn't about to complain about that, especially when all Leif had been left with was an empty house.

With masks firmly back in place, they got out of the cab and she followed him into the store for some major distraction.

An hour and a half later, ten minutes shy of the hardware closing time, they rolled two shopping carts filled to overflowing to the checkout. Gallon after gallon of top-quality mural paints in a dozen different colors plus protective clear varnish to ward off the effects of weather. Primer, which Leif would apply after preparing the walls for her. Every size and shape brush she could possibly need, drop cloths and plastic basins for mixing colors. Thinners. Thickeners. On and on and on the supplies piled up on the counter.

"Oh, we can't forget these," Marta said adding several packages of paint odor valved respirators to the pile.

When the total rang up, Leif didn't blink. Marta tried to not look but noticed anyway and was surprised by the total. "Put it on my account," he said.

Both pushing a cart back to his truck, she couldn't ignore where her thoughts had been heading since they'd walked into the store. "So you're the town benefactor for this project?"

He tried to look surprised but did a poor job of it and immediately came clean. "I made a bundle building that college," he said while opening the tailgate and beginning to unload the supplies. "When the topic came up about the mural, the committee balked at the expense. I volunteered to see it through. That's all."

"I'm being paid very well. You must be a rich man."

"Like I said, I've been blessed with a successful family business."

"That you've obviously grown into a mega business."

He nodded, playing down the blood, sweat and tears that must have gone into the process. "True."

She tapped his chest. "You're far too humble, Leif Andersen."

He laughed. "Not that humble. Truth is, I want this mural to be a kind of legacy for my family. For my father, who added so much to this community, and my mother, who'd always been a patron of the arts. And for my wife, who believed in the community college from the start, when everyone said it was a crazy idea."

"Like I said, you're too humble." As she handed him another can of paint, their gazes clicked with perception and they finished unloading in silence.

One more unsettling thought occurred to Marta as they emptied the carts. There was a huge similarity to his position of benefactor and her recent personal history with Lawrence. Hadn't she vowed to never let that happen again? The difference was, this was a job. She'd been hired. There was nothing personal between them. Though they'd definitely reached a new understanding this afternoon. She'd opened up to him, and he'd opened up to her. They'd shared a special moment in the car.

Something had come over her after hearing his heart-wrenching story, and she couldn't help herself. She'd reached out for him in the parking lot and they'd connected. Spending the afternoon with Leif had been the highlight of her day, and how crazy was that for a pregnant woman?

She was in Heartlandia for a job, and though the city had hired her, Leif was writing the paychecks. No matter how appealing he was, she'd keep everything between her and Leif from here on out strictly professional.

She had no choice.

Chapter Three

It had been four days since Leif had told Marta about his wife and she'd told him about the pregnancy—and they'd shared a special moment. But she'd pulled back. He'd gotten up each morning and left for work before she was awake, though a time or two he'd heard her losing her cookies before he'd left. When he came home, he'd walk the dogs. Inevitably, by the time he'd gotten back she'd have left a note on the kitchen counter saying she'd already eaten and not to cook for her.

Mostly, she'd stayed in her studio. He knew she was working hard at placing the grid on her preliminary mural, but wasn't she getting cabin fever? The most surprising part was how he'd already missed what little interaction they'd had those first couple of days. Here he'd been living as if he didn't need anyone anymore, yet her presence made him hungry for companionship. What was that about?

He didn't think less of her because she was pregnant, but did she think he did? Maybe it mattered to her that he was a man who'd never managed to get his life back on track once he'd lost his wife. Or maybe she felt as though she'd told him too much and wanted to keep things on a different level. He couldn't figure out the change in her by guessing, that was for sure.

One thing he did know—he owed her some kind of explanation about why she was blocked with her painting. It wasn't her imagination; there was a reason and she deserved to hear it, yet he'd kept her dangling in the dark. Sure, there was going to be a town-wide meeting tomorrow morning breaking the news, but why let Marta think she was a little cuckoo for having those weird feelings about the beginning of Heartlandia's history for one more day? Besides, it would give him an excuse to draw her out of the artist's cave.

She was one perceptive woman, and he hoped his reason for asking her to take a ride with him right now wasn't nearly as transparent as he suspected it might be. He missed her and wanted to spend some time with her. Was that a crime? Something about her, besides her good looks, called out to him.

Whatever the reason, it was only three o'clock on a beautiful day. Why not take advantage of it? He rushed up the steps and tapped on the studio door.

"Come in," she said softly.

"Haven't seen you in a while." He entered the studio, aware of the huge mess. "How are you?"

"Doing well."

That was not how she looked. Weren't pregnant women supposed to have some kind of glow or something? She looked pale and tired and maybe even a little thinner than when she'd first arrived. How long was morning sickness supposed to last?

"The grid almost done?"

She nodded. "I'll be ready to go by next week. I'm going to work backward with the painting, like we talked about, and see what happens when I get to the beginning."

"Sounds like a solid plan."

"I'm just not sure how much space to leave."

"I guess that's something to take into consideration."

Her eyes drifted back to the grid with a fretful stare. Maybe he could make her day a little better.

"Oh, hey, I was just thinking it's really nice out and you've kind of been cooped up in here for a few days, and the dogs and I are going to—"

"Sure, I'd love to." She went to the sink and washed her hands.

He cocked his head and suppressed a smile. "How do you know what I'm asking?" Did she always cut people off?

A light, teasing laugh trickled from her lips. It was really great to hear it. "I'm sorry. It's a bad habit, but I was pretty sure you were going to invite me along, right?"

"You happen to know where we're going, too?" He couldn't resist teasing her, and when she laughed at his playful dig, he grinned.

"Maybe I am psychic after all." She smiled for him and the bright studio got even lighter. "Let me get my purse and I'll be right with you."

It felt great to talk to her again, and he looked forward to spending time with her. He planned to take her to his favorite place, a small park just before the Ringmuren where the view of the river was spectacular.

"I'm ready," she said a couple of minutes later, popping out of nowhere, a baggy olive-green sweatshirt over her white work shirt and worn jeans. She'd run a brush through her hair, too, and the sun from the skylights cast a bright sheen over the raven-colored waves.

"Let's go, then."

The view of the Columbia River was magnificent from this vantage point. Marta would have believed it if Leif told her it was the Pacific Ocean because the opposite bank was nowhere in sight. And farther south in the distance, the Astoria-Megler Bridge looked as if it was a hundred miles long. Wow.

She inhaled fresh air and felt less queasy than she had in days. The dogs frolicked around the park without cares, and their antics made her laugh. "Do they ever get tired of chasing that Frisbee?"

"Never," Leif deadpanned and tossed it again.

He struck her as a solid guy, one who carried on no matter how tough the going got. He'd already been through hell; anything else must seem trivial.

"Let's sit over here." He pointed to a bench at the end of a pretty walkway surrounded by flowers. Though it was hard to tear her gaze away from the river, she followed him.

When they arrived, Marta realized the bench was a memorial to Leif's father. "You put this here?"

He nodded. "Dad always liked this view."

After only knowing Leif for a short time, Marta suspected there were a couple other perfectly placed benches in Heartlandia for his mother and wife, too. A pang of sorrow over her mother caught her off guard. Maybe she'd call her father later to catch up. "Well, it certainly is fantastic. This is a lovely part of the country."

"Agreed."

"You've never wanted to leave?"

"I considered it in my late teens, but then my dad offered me the apprenticeship and I had the good sense to recognize a solid future when I saw it. Then after Ellen died, I thought I'd get the hell out of Dodge, but something held me back." He'd been facing the vista, but now he turned and engaged Marta's questioning stare. "All my memories are here, you know? If I left, I'd feel like a huge part of me was missing. Where's a guy supposed to go from there?"

How different that was from her need to break the chains of her overbearing parents when she was a teen. She'd left home for college and never looked back. She'd thought of her mom and dad as old-fashioned and wanted nothing to do with their lifestyle. Leif honored his parents and their memories. She loved and missed her mother and decided right on the spot that when she finished the mural she'd paint a series of pictures dedicated to her. Some might say it was too little too late, but hopefully her father wouldn't be one of them.

"So you get comfort knowing your loved ones once existed here," she said.

He agreed, then tapped his chest. "And here. Always."

"But you take your heart everywhere you go."

"True. But there's actual evidence of my mother and father and Ellen here. I guess I'd worry my memories would fade faster if I went somewhere else."

There was that urge again to reach out and touch him, to take hold of his hand and squeeze, to let the man know he wouldn't always be alone, but could she guarantee it?

At this point in her life, she felt completely alone, too, and the fact she was staying in Leif's house helped smooth out those rough feelings, but there was no guarantee she'd ever find anyone to love again, either.

Something about Leif called out to her. He deserved so much more than what life had dealt him.

"Listen," he said. "I wanted to clear the air about something."

That got her attention. They needed to clear the air already?

"We've recently come to find out our town's story isn't exactly the way our history books tell it."

"What are you talking about?"

"I'm saying there may be a reason you've been artistically blocked at the beginning of your project."

Okay, now he was making the hair on her arms rise, and not in a good way. "Go on."

He proceeded to tell her the whole sordid tale of the Prince of Doom discovering Heartlandia. How he'd shanghaied sailors from Scandinavian ports and forced them to come here. How his ship had sunk and, though it had never been found, may very well still be somewhere off the coast of Heartlandia in the Columbia River.

Then he explained how none of this would have been known if he hadn't discovered the buried trunk when building the City College.

"If the Chinook and Scandinavian fisherman hadn't joined forces to overthrow the pirates, Heartlandia might have been named Princetown."

She could hardly believe her ears. What a wild story! And what a relief it was to know she wasn't crazy, that there really was a reason for her hesitation to start the mural with the Chinook and Scandinavian fishermen working in harmony to build a storybook town.

The bigger questions was, how had the information been suppressed all these years?

"For the past few months I've been involved with a special committee looking into the contents of the trunk and following up with where the journals led. We'd chosen to keep the information to ourselves until we authenticated the journals, dated them and figured out what exactly they meant. We've finally decided the time is right to move ahead with informing the locals, and tomorrow is our first community meeting. Lilly Matsuda, our new journalist, will follow up with a three-part story, explaining everything."

"This is amazing," Marta said, working very hard not to let her jaw drop.

"Tell me about it. Anyway, I hope you'll come with me tomorrow. I'll introduce to you the mayor and city council and show you around the rest of the town, too."

"I wouldn't miss it for the world."

"Okay, then, it's a date. Hey, feel like grabbing something to eat? Oh, wait, I already know the answer to that."

She offered a sad-faced smile. "I wish I had an appetite."

"How about if I make us omelets?"

She tried to look enthusiastic but only managed a wan smile. He read right through it. "I'll make yours as bland as water. You should be able to get some of that down, right?"

She screwed up her face, unsure how the food would affect her. "Sometimes it's more about texture than taste or smell."

"I make great toast, too." The guy was persistent, and

his effort made her want to at least try to eat. He snapped his fingers. "Oh, hey, how about a fruit smoothie?"

She lifted her brows. Ah, now he was on to something. "That has merit. I'll give it my best effort," she said with deep appreciation for his concern.

"That's all I can ask." For one quick moment, his everyday good looks stood out against the backdrop of the darkening sky and the deep river below; the fact that she noticed threw her for a second. She had absolutely no business enjoying his appearance, not in her condition.

His sharp whistle for the dogs snapped her out of the thoughts, and they headed back to the big lonely house on the hill that she could spot all the way across town from the memorial bench at Leif's special park.

The next morning the town was buzzing with interest and maybe a little concern. What could merit a town meeting when they hadn't had one since last year when their former mayor announced his early retirement? Leif considered that some of the businesspeople might wonder if the town was in debt or, worse yet, failing. He'd overheard another group whispering about the effects of the financial downturn on tourist towns such as theirs nationwide.

After introducing Marta to Lilly and Desi Rask, Gerda's granddaughter, he planted her on the adjacent chair to Desi and headed to take his place on the podium with the rest of the committee. Marta was wearing the same black slacks and white blouse she'd worn the day she'd arrived. Looking at her from the podium, there was no way anyone could suspect she was pregnant. Both artists, Desi and Marta, appeared to chat easily while waiting for the event to begin. It made Leif happy to see her connect with new people. He worried he kept her locked up in his empty castle like Rapunzel or something.

Gerda, the mayor pro tem; Elke Norling, the town historian; Gunnar Norling, her brother and local police sergeant; Jarl Madsen from the Maritime Museum; Adamine Olsen, president of the Small Business Association; and Ben Cobowa, the only Native American of Chinook ancestry on the committee, all sat in a unifying row.

The interested crowd grew by the minute, and by ten o'clock, the appointed time for the meeting, the city college auditorium was packed to standing room only.

The mayor stepped to the microphone, her usual white bun twisted so tight, Leif wondered if it would give her a headache. She cleared her throat. "Thank you all for coming." She waited for the chatter to die down, but it didn't.

Gunnar, in his police uniform, stepped forward. "We'd like to get started," he said loudly. "Let's pipe down, okay?" He nudged Gerda back to the podium microphone as the auditorium grew quieter.

"We've called this town meeting to announce some rather startling news we've recently discovered."

Her use of the word *startling* caused the few remaining talkers to go quiet.

"I know you're all anxious to hear why we called everyone here today, so we'll get right to the point. When we broke the ground for the college, Leif Andersen discovered an ancient trunk. The contents were priceless and we have spent the past several months making sure everything was authentic. Elke Norling has done a wonderful job, and we wanted to share the information with you."

From there Gerda went on to tell the story of Captain

Nathaniel Prince to the obvious disbelief of many in the crowd. Several times, Sgt. Norling had to ask the auditorium to pipe down again, and glancing around at the faces, Leif realized the magnitude of this disconcerting news about their beloved town roots.

Adamine Olsen then stood and explained how the local businesses could capitalize on this new information, that the allure of a one-time pirate outpost turned solid small town and sleepy little tourist attraction could be a boon for the local shops and restaurants.

Gerda stressed what mattered most was not how they'd begun but how they'd turned out, and there was nothing to be ashamed of.

Then came the questions of why they'd waited so long to come forth with this information. Gerda tried her best to explain that the committee had wanted to be completely sure about their findings before addressing the town. Leif was grateful she hadn't included the fact he'd sat on his findings several months before bringing it to the town's attention.

Everyone knew Gerda had only stepped in to the mayor position when the town needed a fill-in after their mayor had had a heart attack. She'd done so willingly. What they didn't know was that almost immediately Gerda had gotten slapped with the crazy possibility of the pirate discovering what everyone knew as Heartlandia. The stress had made Gerda sick, but she'd struggled on and led the committee in an honorable way.

"We realize there must be hundreds of questions." Gerda spoke over the grumbling. "And that's why the *Heartlandia Herald* will be running a series of articles beginning this afternoon in a special edition and continuing through Saturday. We want to stress that it's not how you begin that counts, but how you end up, and Heartlandia is still the wonderful place we've all known and loved all of our lives. None of that has changed. So please bear with us. This committee has worked hard to make the best of a troubling situation. If after the series of articles your questions are still unanswered, please feel free to submit any and all questions to the newspaper. We vow to answer each and every one personally as well as in the newspaper.

"The most important thing to take away today is that our town hasn't changed. We are still the great town of Heartlandia. The only change is how we got started. Please continue to be proud to be a citizen of the best little place on the Oregon coast."

The questions flew from the curious and agitated crowd, but there was no point in sticking around because the first newspaper article would hit the stands that afternoon. Lilly had done a phenomenal job of writing the articles, and the entire committee had approved them. They'd printed triple the usual copies, expecting a run on the newspaper.

As far as Leif was concerned the meeting was over. He left the stage, grabbed a stunned-looking Marta by the arm and took her out a side exit.

"I had no idea how this would affect the citizens. It didn't seem like such a big deal to me," she said. "Wow. This is crazy."

"All we can do is move forward. Paint your mural from present day to the beginning. I'm sure you'll figure out how to portray this part when you get there."

"I certainly hope so." She didn't look the least bit confident, and Leif decided distraction was the key to helping her relax.

"Come on. I'm going to rent you a car so you can have more freedom. You must be going bonkers being stuck in my house all day."

Her eyes lit up. "That's a great idea, but I can rent my own car."

He gave her a "don't argue with me" look, the kind that imparted there was no way in hell she'd win this debate. She inhaled, ready for a fight, thinking how her parents used to give her ultimatums all the time, but wasn't Leif completely different, only thinking of her welfare? *Hmm, maybe that's all they'd been thinking about, too.* Mentally shaking her head at her old headstrong self, wishing she could turn back the clock, she accepted his offer.

Using the GPS, Marta spent the next few days exploring the city and getting to know some of the townsfolk. Though everyone, and she meant everyone, was in an uproar about the crazy news—she'd kept up with the three-part story like everyone else, and found them extremely well written, informative and to the point—she was still enchanted by Heartlandia. What a wonderful place it was. Who cared if some crazy pirate discovered the land?

The Chinook and the Scandinavian fishermen had worked together to build the town…after they'd joined forces to overthrow the pirates. What city worth its salt didn't have a dab of violence in its past? She chuckled quietly and shook her head. Who'd believe this from looking at the city today?

Rethinking what Mayor Rask had said—what mattered most was how the town had wound up, not how it had begun—Marta scouted out a parking space. Wasn't that a lesson for everyone? She'd been calling home just about every night talking to her dad, sharing what was going on in her life but conveniently leaving out the part about being pregnant. That was something she preferred to tell him face-to-face. If she kept up these calls, maybe she'd work up the courage to tell him how sorry she was for the way she'd treated them way back then. Sure, she'd been a royal pain to her parents, but what mattered most was how she'd turned out—pretty darn well, thank you very much. Hopefully her father would understand that point. She just wished her mother could be around for the long-overdue apology.

The scent of fresh bread wafted through her opened window, and fond memories of her mother's kitchen piggybacked along. There went another pang of sadness and loss. Being pregnant made a woman think about her own mother a lot. The inviting smell continued to invade her nostrils as she parked in front of a little bakery with a blue-and-white canopy. She took a deep breath and realized for the first time in three months she wasn't queasy. Rushing out of the car she went inside and, seizing the moment, she ordered a fresh croissant, then slathered it with butter and jam. She nearly inhaled it. God, she was hungry.

And not the least bit nauseous.

Thinking *what the heck* because she didn't know how long her reprieve might last, she ordered a second croissant. Once she'd wolfed that down, she asked for directions from the clerk and headed to the nearest market. A huge weight had lifted from her. She was almost through with the first trimester, and could the loss of nausea possibly be ahead of schedule? All she knew for sure was today, this hour, her appetite had returned, and, boy, had she missed it.

After two weeks of Leif cooking for this very picky eater, it was about time for payback. Because she still felt great, she decided he deserved a special dinner prepared especially for him.

Off she went to buy the ingredients to her favorite Tex-Mex, Sedona-style meal, hoping Leif would enjoy every bite. Fingers crossed she'd keep her appetite through dinner.

Leif came home from a long hard day of construction to the most amazing smells. Meat, onions, spices and corn tortillas. He entered the kitchen to a busy and beautiful Marta wearing a forgotten apron and whisking around his kitchen with three pots simmering on the stove.

"Hi!" she said brightly.

"Wow. What's all this?"

"I'm finally hungry, and this is my way of saying thank-you for taking such good care of me."

He couldn't help the smile as he lifted one of the lids and took a deep inhale. "This smells great."

"I was hoping you'd say that. It's beef and wheatberry chili, just like my momma used to make. Now wash your hands, pour yourself a glass of wine and grate some cheese for me, okay? I had to improvise with Colby-Jack since the clerk gave me a blank stare when I asked where the queso was."

"What do you expect from Little Scandinavia?"

"Good point."

How could a guy refuse a beautiful lady with a wooden spoon in one hand and a small plate of diced green chiles in the other? She had poured herself a tall glass of lemonade and it looked so good, he decided to forgo the wine and join her. As Leif poured his drink, the fatigue of the day lifted, and because of Marta's contagious happy mood he thought he might be smiling all through dinner.

And so went the next few days—Leif came home to meals already on the stovetop or in the oven. One night she'd surprised him after dinner with mint-chip ice cream sandwiched between two extralarge homemade chocolate-chip cookies.

Another night she'd made pasta sauce that tasted as good as his own. After they'd washed the dishes together, like a carefree kid he'd picked up three tangerines from a bowl on the counter and juggled for her—a trick he'd learned in high school specifically to impress girls. Then he memorized the surprise and joy on her face as she clapped and tolerated his out-of-character antics. Since when had he enjoyed himself enough with anyone to let part of his old self sneak out?

One night, deciding to have a glass of wine with dinner—another excellent meal from his houseguest— he was surprised when his mind wandered to a quick fantasy of cooking a meal with Marta.

That wasn't where those thoughts ended, either. Night after night he'd torn up his bed in fitful sleep, once waking in the middle of a hot and sexy dream where he was wrapped in the body of a faceless woman. It had to stop. He couldn't let himself become a sad and foolish bore pretending that this "thing" going on with Marta was anything more than a business proposition. One she'd agreed to take for pay.

The fact he'd spent several nights restlessly staring at the ceiling, wanting things he'd forced himself to forget and imagining how empty the house would feel again after she left, nearly sent him over the edge. He needed to get hold of himself. There was nothing between them beyond two people learning to cope with what life had thrown at them. They'd achieved a comfortable rhythm in their day-to-day life, and the last thing he wanted to do was ruin it.

Thursday night, Leif sat at Cliff Lincoln's bar nursing a beer after a long day. He inhaled and chewed his lower lip, trying his damnedest to get Marta's face, her sculptured nose, cheeks and chin, and especially her soft, plump lips, out of his mind. He'd purposely avoided going home tonight after the crazy, sexy dream he'd had last night. In it, he was making love again, and this time he'd seen her, couldn't deny who it was. Her long artful fingers had stroked his skin, driving him to wake up hard as cement.

He downed the last of his drink, dreading coming face to face with her later, and by the time he got home, she was already upstairs. He presumed it was for the night. An odd mix of relief and regret circulated through his brain. Nowhere near ready for bed, he considered lighting a fire, but the thought of just having the dogs to share it with seemed all wrong. Instead, he decided to take Chip and Dale for one last moonlit walk.

An hour later, he headed up the stairs.

"Leif? Is that you?"

Pleasantly surprised she was still up at ten o'clock, he wandered to her studio. "Yeah. It's me." It was great to see her in her loose lounging pants and with a colorful purple scarf tied around her head.

"I'm heating some water for some herbal tea. Want to join me?"

"Sure." He wasn't about to refuse an invitation to spend more time with the woman he'd been trying all night to get out of his mind. Because he really was a sap.

"I'm glad you're here. I wanted to show you something."

He walked closer, trying his hardest not to notice her cinnamon and ginger scent.

"What do you think?" He glanced at her and liked what he saw. Oh, wait...she was asking about something else.

She'd filled in the blank, as it were, and added a front portion to her mural. It was mostly a striking landscape of the Columbia River, cliffs, rocks and all. In the center sat a ship painted to scale. It looked small compared to the raging river but was big enough to figure out Neptune's Fortune belonged to Nathaniel Prince. Subtle yet telling, the perfect balance of truth and suppression.

"I like it."

"Do I need to get approval from your committee?"

"It would be a good idea to run this by them, but I can't think of any protests. It gets the point across without hitting anyone over the head."

"That's exactly what I was going for." She looked appreciatively at him and they shared another one of those instants where the tension tugged between them, the kind of moment that seemed to happen more and more often. Her expression changed quickly from mere appreciation to something more, and there went that longing, straight from his gut. Again. Thank God the kettle whistled and broke things up or he might have done something he'd regret.

Soon, she was sipping her piping hot tea and studying him, while he blew on his. He wasn't the least bit comfortable under her scrutiny. "What?"

Caught in her obvious stare, she smiled. "You, that's what. I'm glad to see you, that's all."

Well, because she was sharing, he felt compelled to be honest. "I have to admit, for the first time in ages, all this past week I've looked forward to coming home." Except for tonight when he wasn't ready to face her after having such a lifelike erotic dream about her.

"Because the house isn't empty."

Was that the reason? "Maybe."

"Did you have to work late tonight?" So matter of fact. He wasn't used to people being this straightforward.

"Had some things I had to do." It wasn't a lie if what he'd "had" to do was sit in a bar, have a beer and think about what he should do about all the crazy feelings he'd developed for Marta.

"I have to admit I like it better when you're here at night. This place is so quiet otherwise." She went back to studying the latest section of the painting.

"You can always bring Chip and Dale in to keep you company, you know." She seemed to enjoy the dogs, but maybe she wasn't a dog person like he was.

"That's a good idea. Next time you work late, I'll do that."

Things changed. She'd shown him the new part of the mural and maybe that was all she wanted. Aware she was deep in thought, he felt as if he needed to leave, but it was the last thing he wanted to do, so he stood there staring at her, thinking how lovely she was, watching her long slender fingers measure and sketch within the grid. Enjoying her hips as she bent over to draw. He forced himself to look away and blew over the tea again. It wasn't just the tea that needed to cool off.

"Is that what your wife used to do?"

His mind had wandered far from the subject, and the insertion of his wife into the conversation threw him. Was she making a point? "Pardon?" Had he been too obvious? Great going, idiot.

"When you worked long hours, did Ellen use the dogs for companionship?"

Obviously, Marta was reminding him he had a wife he still mourned. Or was she challenging him? "She had a lot of friends and also kept busy with her projects. Though the dogs were always good company. The good part about owning your own company is you can set the rules and hours."

Marta had gone still, as if she'd had far too much time to think this evening and was thinking extra hard right now. Anyone in their right mind could figure out he was way out of practice with women. She'd also lived in this house long enough to sense it was a huge mausoleum instead of a home. He was stuck here and couldn't move forward. And wasn't that why he was so damn mixed up about the sexy dreams and the desire to spend time with this outsider, the artist from Sedona?

She stood with her freshly brewed tea, walked around the worktable, balanced a hip on the edge, then took a sip. "How come you've never—"

Radar, intuition, whatever he wanted to call it, he knew exactly what she was asking. "Remarried?" She wasn't the only one who could read minds and cut people off midsentence. Hell, he'd only taken off his ring last year. "Because I can't imagine ever replacing her. I don't see how anyone can ever measure up. No woman wants to settle for replacement status." His tea was still too hot to drink easily, but he forced a swallow, roof of mouth be damned.

"So your alternative is to keep yourself locked up in this gorgeous prison of a house."

He didn't like where this conversation was going and made no bones about showing Marta his negative reaction. "I have a job, and I go out every day. I'm hardly locked up here." Why did he feel so defensive? Because she was challenging him.

"True, but not convincing." She leveled her gaze to his, and he wanted to squirm out of it. "The difference between you and me is that I've never turned my back on love. Loving comes easily for me. It always has. Isn't that the point of being on this planet? We're here to share love with each other."

Oh, yeah, here she went with all that free spirit Sedona mumbo jumbo. He looked at her differently now, wondering how many relationships she'd been in during her adult life. "The thing is, you have to find the right person to share love. Otherwise it's not really love, is it?"

"That may be true, but sometimes jerks, if given the chance, turn out to be the most wonderful people." She glanced wistfully up through the skylight, where a gibbous moon was rising. "And sometimes the most wonderful men turn out to be jerks," she said softly, with a resigned tone.

He wanted to get angry for her broaching a tough topic at the drop of a hat, but instead he fought that constant urge to comfort her, to wrap her in his arms and let her know she didn't have to be alone. He was here for her.

Yet he didn't move. Couldn't.

Because wasn't that crazy? He'd just assured her that any woman in his life would merely be a replacement, that he'd closed the door on any future relationship because it wouldn't be fair. He shouldn't be having these kinds of feelings. He wasn't ready. Would probably never be.

Aware he hadn't uttered a response, she nailed him with those dark, inquisitive eyes.

"You might think of me as a fool, but even now I'm optimistic I'll love again. I wouldn't be alive otherwise."

Wait a minute—had she just lobbed a sly attack? "So because I'm not in love or planning to fall in love, that makes me dead?" He was distracted by her beauty and at the same time irritated she was hitting him with tough reality. And the last thing he wanted to do was have this conversation.

"I'm not calling you anything. I'm just sharing how I feel about love and life. I make no judgment on you."

She was digging too close to raw nerves, and he ground his molars rather than spit out the first thought in his head. *You have no idea what I went through.* But he did wonder what she was getting at, and for some crazy reason it mattered what she thought. "You think I'm a ghost? You think I don't feel?"

She shook her head widely. "I know you feel. I've been around you long enough to know you are a kind and sensitive man. You've opened your home to me. You've made me feel like a special guest." She bit her lower lip and with soft, inquiring eyes she probed. "I'm just thinking it would be such a waste to never love again. As brokenhearted as I am right now, I still look forward to the opportunity to fall head over heels again. It gives me hope." She set down her tea, then on an inhale she must have formed one more thought. "Knowing that I'm open to new relationships helps me through the rough places. There's something out there waiting for me. All I have to do is find them."

Still bristling from her earlier comments, now reeling from this revelation and all mixed-up inside, he shifted uncomfortably from one foot to the other. She stood before him beautiful, radiant, filled with life, and that naked dream with her straddling him, touching him everywhere flashed in his brain.

She was open to love. What the hell was that supposed to mean?

"I'm just wondering what helps you survive," she said.

He'd barely been surviving, as it turned out, and the first woman forced into his life had quickly become a fantasy driving him crazy. He wanted her, and he couldn't utter a sound or she'd figure it out.

"Are you just surviving?" she prodded.

What was with the interrogation? Who was she to point out how badly he'd handled his losses? He ran a business. Had a home. Owned dogs. He lived and breathed.

Damn it. He *was* just surviving.

"There's more to life than surviving, Leif."

That was it—she'd crossed the line. She viewed his life as mere survival. She talked as if she knew him and understood his circumstances, which she didn't. No one could. How could he pick up the pieces and move on when they'd been scattered so far he could never find them?

So why in the hell was he still so damned attracted

to Marta, even though she'd pried far too deep and kept pushing and pushing?

Instead of feeling furious, as part of him felt he had the right be, he got waylaid by the growing desire that had kept him awake the past week simply by having Marta under his roof. That feeling finally hit full force. If he was going to feel guilty as hell for lusting after her, he may as well have a damn good reason. In the next second, as if a dam of pent-up feelings, building and battling for release, had sprung a leak, he lost it.

Completely confused but driven by his gut reaction, Leif put down his tea with a thud, hot liquid splashing over the lip, burning his hand, but he didn't care. If she wanted to know what surviving looked like, he was about to show her. With three long strides and a boatload of determination, he grabbed Marta by her arms, pulled her close and kissed her.

Marta felt the intensity coursing through Leif's pulse. All passion without a hint of finesse, his mouth pressed hard and ragged against hers, and she let him. Didn't even consider fighting him. Stunned into submission, she allowed the kiss to pound through her, deeper and deeper still, bewildered by the stirring he'd set off inside. His claiming lips made her knees weaken and her insides quiver. She put her arms around his solid shoulders and held on tight for the wildest kiss of her life.

Yes. She kissed him back. She wasn't ashamed to admit she was as attracted to him as he obviously was to her. Her philosophy in life had always been things happen for a purpose.

But as abruptly as the kiss had started, he ended it, his eyes dancing over every part of her when he did, heat flaming inside them, communicating two perfect thoughts.

You asked for it. Had she?

And *I bet you didn't see that coming, Miss Psychic.* No. She definitely hadn't.

Oh, but there was so much more in that burrowing stare. He'd lost his battle for control, and he wasn't sorry. His kiss had made her brain mush and left her body tingling.

Before she could think one more thought, and long before she could ever hope to form a single word, he bid her good-night, turned and left the studio, closing the door with a thud behind him.

Standing perfectly still, catching her breath, taking stock of her full-bodied reaction, she realized she'd moistened her underwear...from one rough and heady kiss.

She tried to swallow but couldn't, so she reached for her tea and lifted it with trembling fingers. "My God," she whispered after taking a sip. "What just happened?"

She'd taunted a beast out of its cage and the result had been indescribable. Could she even call that a kiss? His hungry mouth had clamped onto hers and sent her parasailing through the skylight. She wrapped an arm around her stomach, trying her best to regain some balance.

She'd lectured him, a man who'd chosen to shut himself away from that part of his life for three years, about not giving up on love. Used herself as an example. Dangled the higher, mightier approach in the face of an emotionally starving man, knowing full well he'd been traumatized by loss.

Had she bullied him into kissing her?

And now that she'd unleashed his sexual outburst, where did they go from here?

Marta inhaled a shaky breath, knowing without a doubt she'd be up all night trying to figure out the odd yet powerful chemistry she and Leif Andersen most definitely shared. Plus the fact she'd promised herself to keep this relationship purely professional. Still knowing without a doubt that if he ever wanted to kiss her again, she'd let him.

So much for promises.

Chapter Four

Six o'clock Friday morning, Leif stood in the kitchen making a pot of coffee, the only light from filtered rays of frail early Oregon sun. He hadn't slept most of the night, warring with the onslaught of feelings he'd unleashed. He and Marta couldn't continue to stay under the same roof after that kiss last night. If he couldn't control a kiss, there was no telling what might happen next. How must she feel? Hopefully not violated. He wouldn't blame her if she asked to move out, though.

If only things were different.

A quiet rustling behind him drew his attention. He turned. It was Marta. And there went that same tiny implosion he experienced every time he saw her.

"I'm sorry," they said in unison.

"No," he said. "It was all my fault. Forgive me."

"I was equally responsible." She was wearing that

Southwest-patterned robe again and her hair hadn't come near a brush, and the effect made him immediately lose his resolve to steer clear of her. "And honestly, I'm not sure apologies are even in order," she said, tossing her hair and lifting her chin. "We may have been thrown together for a specific purpose with the mural, but who knows why else?"

Her logic evaded him. He didn't think in such esoteric ways. *Why else?* Sounded like Sedona mumbo jumbo for that meant-to-be baloney spouted by romantics. One thing was sure—he was not a romantic. At least she wasn't taking the sexual harassment route. What a mess.

When in doubt, play dense.

"Your point being?" Suddenly dying for his first taste of coffee, anything to distract him from her, and needing fortification to make the slightest bit of sense out of her "who knows why else" statement, he poured and drank.

"Sometimes things are meant to happen. Maybe we've met for a reason." She kept her distance and leaned against the door frame with her arms folded, studying his face as if preparing to sketch him.

With her explanation the world seemed far too complicated to navigate. "It's way too early for me to think, let alone wrap my brain around that, Marta."

A quick smile creased her lips. "I'm pretty sure thinking had nothing to do with what happened last night."

Wasn't that the truth! That moment of insanity, kissing her as if it might be his last kiss ever, thrummed through him. He had to make things right.

"Look, I can arrange to store Gunnar and Lilly's things and move into the guesthouse if—"

"Not at all necessary on my account. Please." Those

pleading chocolate eyes made their point without further words.

She was okay with what had happened.

There was no need to ask if she was sure or not; the tilt of her chin settled it. He drank her in with the next sip of coffee. She was fine with things as they were. "Okay. But keep in mind you may be too intuitive for your own good."

He poured more coffee into his travel mug and headed out the door to take the dogs for a quick walk. Once he'd let off steam, he'd go right on to work. The less he saw of Marta right now, the more in control he'd feel, and he definitely needed to take back some control.

But as the day wore on, his strategy didn't pan out. He thought about Marta spending too much time on her project. He worried about the baby. Was Marta eating the way pregnant women should? Was she getting enough rest? And though they'd apologized to each other that morning, it didn't feel official enough. He should do something more. To distract himself from the barrage of thoughts, he worked hard right along with the crew putting the finishing touches on Gunnar's house. As he did, an idea for multitasking occurred to him.

"Rick and Dexter, I want you guys to head over to the college and start scraping off the stucco on those bungalows we talked about in the history quad." The only way to keep Marta out of his hair—and mind—was to keep her busy and out of the house. The sooner he prepped those cement walls for her, the sooner she could begin painting her mural and—though he hated to think about the next part, it was necessary—the sooner she would leave town.

End of problem.

The intuitive artist made him squirm with feelings that for three years he'd managed to keep at bay. She could recite all that "meant to be" business as much as she wanted, but he wasn't buying it. Nope. She was a beautiful woman and he'd fallen for her looks. That was all. He was nothing but a shallow man and her beauty had done him in.

But what about her quiet ways and how it calmed him knowing that she was at work in the studio? What about the energy she'd added to the big empty house? Ack. He pounded a nail into submission, then used a framing nail gun to zip through the rest. The loud and distracting compressor tools were his friends today, as they had been on many rough days in his life.

By lunch, the demanding physical activity had drained the tough-guy barriers right out of him. He felt raw and real, and as he ate a sub sandwich, Marta crept back into his thoughts.

Not the sexy-vixen Marta, but the pregnant, fresh-from-a-broken-relationship version. His vulnerable and appealing houseguest. That line of thought needed to stop. He jutted out his jaw, took another ravenous bite of his sandwich, then put his lunch away and went back to pounding nails and using his drill and power tools, thankful they required his undivided attention to detail.

It didn't work.

Marta's unguarded, wide-eyed expression, bordered with bed hair, planted itself into his mind. Sage or seductress? And why was everything about her so damn appealing?

He tossed his hammer on some nearby grass. "You guys finish up today. I've got an errand to do." He grabbed the towel he kept with his gear and wiped his face and neck. Then, secure in his handpicked crew finishing the job without supervision, he headed to his truck.

He'd become a pro at shopping for healthy groceries when his wife had first been diagnosed. He also knew the perfect power-food soup that, if good for a cancer patient, must be guaranteed to increase a baby's IQ and boost a mother's vigor. Off he went to the supermarket with a mental list already prepared.

By four o'clock he was cleaned up and standing in front of the stove stirring vegetable stock, adding chopped this and that and finally the skinless, boneless chicken he'd cut into bite-size pieces and browned in a pan. He'd also stopped by the bakery and bought some fresh dark rye bread, which was still warm and smelled great.

Forty-five minutes later, Marta hadn't stirred from her studio, so he carried a tray with two bowls of soup and a basket of bread with butter up the stairs. Nothing said "I'm sorry *and* I hope you're taking care of yourself" like a healthy home-cooked meal.

Testing a new color, Marta heard a faint tap on the door. "Come in!"

Leif used his shoulder to push through the door. He emerged with a tray of food, and because Marta hadn't eaten in a few hours, the aroma set her stomach juices to dancing. Well, that and the natural-born male delivering it. "What's this?"

"My special power-play soup. You're gonna love it."

"If you say so." She'd always liked confident men, and on so many levels Leif fit the bill—except when it came to venturing toward her. What a sweet gesture, though. "Wow, it looks great."

He put the tray on the kitchenette sink and delivered both bowls to the small table in the corner. "Let's eat, then."

Blowing over her spoon with the first bite, watching Leif do the same across from her, she was touched. His thoughtfulness seemed so different from the crazed-with-lust man who'd kissed the air out of her last night. This was the Leif she'd first found so appealing—the earnest, caring guy who'd been dealt a lousy hand in life. But the man she'd encountered last night was what'd sealed the deal for her on the concept of Scandinavian lovers. Roll both men together and, wow, she felt like the luckiest girl in the world…that was, the luckiest single pregnant woman in Heartlandia.

Maybe she needed to put a little more thought into this. Besides her being in the family way, the man was an emotional landmine, which until last night she'd only suspected, and now she knew for sure. She wasn't doing so great in that department lately, either, and she was definitely in no condition to deal with *those* feelings right now. She had a job to do—a big job. The biggest job of her professional life. And the most important.

So much for her meant-to-be philosophy. Not this time. She'd said it to him without realizing the extent of Leif's issues, and in that regard, boy, had she been wrong for so many reasons. The two most obvious being she was pregnant and he was still mourning his wife.

Their timing was colossally off for any kind of potential relationship. Sad but true.

"You should market this soup. It's fantastic," she said, hoping to put her mind back on food instead of the overwhelmingly appealing man across from her. Especially after her compliment when his proud, sexy grin nearly undid her.

"I told you. This is going to make that baby do somersaults."

"Oh, gosh, I hope not. I've just only gotten my appetite back." She gave a self-deprecating smile, knowing how much they'd shared over nearly four weeks and how generous he'd been throughout. "The last thing I need is my baby rolling around inside."

He grinned again, genuine and handsome, and it cut right into her heart.

What in the world was she going to do for the rest of the time it would take to paint the mural?

After another bite, she sat straight. "I've been thinking about your offer of the guesthouse."

She could have sworn there was a flash of disappointment darkening his gaze, but he covered it well and pasted on a smile. "You stay in the house. I'll move out there. It will only take a couple of days before Gunnar and Lilly are ready to take their furniture back to their new house anyway."

"That isn't necessary. This is your house. All I have to do is move my suitcases."

"The suite and studio suit you. You should stay and I'll—"

"You know what? That's just a bad idea. Neither of us should go. Forget I ever said anything."

"But the last thing I want is to know I've made you uncomfortable or that I've kept you locked away in this house if you don't want to be here."

The way you keep your heart? "You've rented a car for me, remember? I can come and go as I please. I don't feel the least bit like a prisoner. I've just been concentrating on the mural preparation, that's all."

"Good." He looked down to the last of his soup, which he sopped up with a chunk of brown bread.

This man was so honest and real. So thoughtful even under fire. Overcome with sweet feelings, she reached out and touched his arm, his gaze quickly finding hers. Then, overcome with his vulnerable side and wanting more, she stood and walked to his side, bent down and delivered a gentle kiss on his stubbled cheek. "Thank you for everything," she whispered.

He looked up, an entire story written in those aqua-blue eyes, yet his mouth was set tight, as if trying not to respond to her kiss.

She couldn't help but suspect his thoughts and repeat them out loud. "If only things were different, right, Leif?"

He cleared his throat and on an inhale stood, wordlessly gathered the dishes and placed them on the tray. In a completely different manner from last night, he solemnly left the room, his response to her query left unspoken.

Three days later, after barely making contact with each other over the weekend and his treating her respectfully but only as an acquaintance whenever they did pass in the hallway, she'd had enough. Early Monday afternoon, he was out back with his dogs filling their water bowl, having just returned from a walk. She rushed out the kitchen door, leaving it flapping behind her, and approached him.

"Hi!"

He turned, looking surprised. Had they made a silent

agreement to keep clear? No! Not her, but it certainly had been his recent approach to their relationship.

"What's up?" he said, affably enough but far from personal.

"I was wondering if you'd take me somewhere."

His brows came together, and he surreptitiously glanced toward her rental car with a puzzled expression. She couldn't let on how angry she'd been with him for completely withdrawing after they'd forged a pretty decent friendship. So what if a couple of kisses confused things? They could still be friends, couldn't they? Truth was, she'd missed his company.

"After reading all of those great articles and learning about the Chinook burial ground in Heartlandia's changing history, I want to see the Ringmuren. And who better to see it with than a town native? Will you take me?"

"Sure." With his chin tucked, he didn't exactly look enthusiastic, but it was a start. "How about tomorrow? I'll let the crew know I won't be around."

She stood straight, unfolding her arms with palms up to communicate she really wanted to spend time with him. "I'd like that." She wasn't sure whether or not her thoughts or actions fell on fertile soil or desert, but she'd done her best to make her point. *Let's spend more time together.* And that would have to be good enough for now.

Tuesday morning, meeting at the agreed-upon time, she'd dressed in her favorite jeans, which were beginning to get too tight around the waist, and a colorful loose top to hide the fact she'd left the top snap on her jeans undone. She'd combed her hair and twisted it around off her neck and splashed an extra drop of her favorite fragrance, a combination of lavender and pumpkin-pie spices, on her shoulders and nape.

He'd also cleaned up nicely, freshly shaved, hair still damp and close to his head, a button-up tailored shirt in a minty green wreaking havoc with his blue eyes and broken-in jeans showing his long, solid legs in all their glory. All man. The grooves on his cheeks deepened with his genuine, greeting smile.

"Ready?" he asked.

"Absolutely."

They drove in companionable silence. The higher up the mountain they went, the greener things got. She spotted Hjartalanda Peak, and he verified it when she pointed it out. Maybe it was the fresh air or the gorgeous scenery, but Marta felt her heart lift and suddenly she had an overwhelming desire to open up to Leif. Hey, they'd known each other a month already, hadn't they? In her opinion it was well past time.

"When I was a little girl, my grandfather used to make a big deal about my drawings." She did her best to imitate how he puffed out his chest and made his eyes big as teacups. "'You are going to be an artist, *mi hija*.'" She also copied his accent, then lightly laughed. Leif turned and smiled along with her.

"Maybe because my grandfather didn't inherit the gift his father had for art, he always encouraged any little attempt I made at drawing and painting. He probably hoped the talent had skipped a generation or two. Whatever. But I believed him and from then on, that's what I wanted to be."

"He was right. You're a gifted painter."

"Thank you. I've worked hard at my craft."

"I can't wait to see the finished mural at the college. And, oh, I've been meaning to tell you the walls are all prepped and you're free to start any time you want."

She wondered if it was because he wanted the assignment completed so she'd get out of his life, but she pushed the thought away. Negativity wasn't her style. Yet she kept waffling back and forth whether she had met Leif for a reason or not. Sometimes she was sure of it; other times she couldn't imagine him ever letting someone into his life again. Why bang her head against his proverbial wall? But he'd offered his house to a stranger, and once that door was open, it was anyone's guess what their ending might be. Today, instead of dwelling on the "not gonna happens" in life, she opted to go with hope. Who knew how things might turn out?

A few minutes later they pulled off the road into an old parking lot covered in gravel, with weeds and flowers growing through jagged cracks in areas of ancient asphalt, a huge expanse of bright green grass just on the other side. A few rocks and boulders erupted through the pristine lawn here and there, giving it a rugged appearance. Gentleman as always, Leif helped her out of the truck cab and they began their trek to this side of the Ringmuren. In the distance she glanced at the long rock-and-stone wall that demarcated the park side from the sacred side. She couldn't wait to get close enough to see the three-hundred-year-old workmanship and what lay beyond. She'd definitely add this wall to the mural.

"Wow, this is gorgeous."

"It is something, isn't it?"

"I can almost feel the history that must have taken place here." The fine hair at the back of her neck stood straight. "This is amazing." Drawing closer, the wall became even more impressive. "They didn't even use mortar to hold this wall together. How has it withstood the elements all these years?"

"Good question. Our Chinook citizens are positive the spirits from the sacred burial ground watch over this wall. We've had some fierce storms over the years, but the wall always stands strong. It's kind of a mystery, when you think about it."

"You're giving me chills." She skimmed her palms over her arms.

"I don't mean to scare you or anything."

"Oh, no. On the contrary. I find this fascinating." She walked on, exploring the wall and peeking over it from the beautifully manicured side to the other rugged and left-to-its-own-resources side. The sacred burial ground. For several moments she stood there, studying and wondering. Leif courteously gave her space to go inward and she imagined the past, how the Scandinavian sailors had joined forces with the Chinook to delineate hallowed from natural ground. How the endeavor must have forged new respect and cooperation between the two groups. How they'd used that respect to go up against the pirates. To fight for their lives and their families.

When she'd thought long and hard enough, adding new vision and a few extra details to her mural, she turned and smiled widely at him. "Thank you for bringing me here. If I ever run out of inspiration, I'll come here to refuel."

"Sounds like a plan."

They walked together toward a group of trees and a small clearing where another bench sat. This one turned out to be dedicated to Leif's mother, Hannah. It was exquisitely carved from a huge tree stump, and the workmanship both touched and impressed her. It made her think of her own mother, Gabriella, and there went that usual pang in her heart for her.

They sat in silence for several minutes, Leif with his legs outstretched and his feet crossed at the ankles, his arms lounging across the back of the rugged bench.

A few moments later he cleared his throat. "You know, I've always envied people who could put their feelings into art."

"And I've always envied people who could build beautiful houses." She shared another smile with him, his eyes picking up the color of the distant Columbia River, and felt warmth spread across her chest. "By the way, who carved the intricate work on your mantel around your fireplace?" She already had a hunch about the answer.

He used his thumb and index fingers and touched the edges of his mouth. "I did."

"Uh-huh, and what about this bench? It looks similar in style. Is this your work, too?"

He dipped his head.

She tapped his thigh. "How can you not consider yourself an artist? Your work is beautiful and like nothing I've ever seen."

He quirked a brow. "You really think so?"

"I know so, but it doesn't matter what I think. What matters is how you feel about it. You need to shape up and admit that you, Leif Andersen, are a gifted craftsman and wood artist."

Obviously trying not to show his pride, he still looked tickled and a little doubtful. "I do enjoy it. I like to leave a special touch in every house I build. Like the bookcase I'm installing at Gunnar's house. It's kind of like my signature."

"It's a good signature. An artist's signature." She smiled just before a somber veil dropped over her expression.

"My mother used to worry being an artist was not the right kind of profession for a young woman. I fought her on it, pushed for my independence. Pushed her away." Marta glanced at her folded hands in her lap. "I wasn't at her side when she died, and to this day I regret all the thoughtless things I said to her. She couldn't understand how I lived. I bragged I never wanted to get married, that it would hold me back." She quietly shook her head. "How that must have hurt her, a woman who wanted nothing more than a loving family, could only have one child, and she got me."

Leif comforted her with a squeeze of her folded hands. "I'm sure she was proud of you."

"I hope so, but I'm afraid all I ever brought her was shame."

"I don't believe that for a minute."

"If she knew I was pregnant and unmarried now, I think she'd roll over in her grave."

He laughed gently at her absurd remark.

"Forgive me for getting all dramatic, but sitting on your mother's bench, well, it made me think of her."

Leif glanced at Marta, happy she appreciated his brand of creativity yet sorry for her complicated, conflicted feelings about her mother, especially not being able to say goodbye before she had died. The sun glinted off her dark hair, making it look silky and touchable. He fought the urge to reach out and roll a loose lock of her hair through his thumb and fingers. How good it used to feel to touch his wife whenever he wanted, to have free reign of her body. What was it about Marta that always led his mind in that direction?

He pulled back his thoughts, worried that Marta really

could read them, but evidently not soon enough. Before
he realized what she was doing, she'd scooted closer on
the bench, her pupils wide and round, her hand reaching for and soon caressing his cheek. Maybe she'd read
his thoughts after all. Without thinking further he tilted
his head and, boom, she kissed him.

Her mouth settled on top of his, spreading warmth
and a gentle invitation to kiss her back. Her sweet, spicy
scent combined with the feel of her plump lips made for
a heady swell. He returned the kiss and soon pressed his
tongue into her welcoming mouth. Her slick, wet tongue
tasted like mint and honey.

He'd missed this part of his life. Being with a woman,
sharing natural responses.

Her sweet, innocent gesture quickly changed to something more. Something about Marta, having her in his
arms, made him come alive. His hands gripped her shoulders and wandered around her back, sizing up her softness and strength. He wondered about how right this
could be. A quick, fanciful thought.

As though sensing his discovery, she responded to
his touch and kissed more eagerly, her fingers pulling
his neck and head closer, the tips pressing into his skin.
It felt great to be wanted. Beyond great. It had been far
too long. But the moment of closeness also brought back
a rush of memories, both good and bad. Opening up
had become too hard, forgotten even. He couldn't allow
himself to get involved. His loss with Ellen had been
too much. He couldn't go there again. It was too painful.

Her sweet kisses were an invitation to heartache and
devastation, and he'd already had more than a lifetime's
worth.

Allowing his torn thoughts to ruin the moment, he

backed away from the kiss, an old, familiar deadness taking hold inside, and he slowly withdrew.

Her puzzled expression soon turned to concern.

She lowered her head, unable to look him in the eyes, his detached attitude shattering her normally straightforward approach. He hated himself for doing that to her but was nowhere near able to explain why he'd done it, knowing without a doubt the old "it's not you, it's me" routine would fall on deaf ears. She'd never buy it. She expected too much of him—expected him to be normal again. Didn't she get that he couldn't?

"It's because I'm pregnant, isn't it?"

What? No! He hadn't even allowed himself to get past the point of kissing a new woman, let alone to think about anything else. The pregnancy hadn't entered his mind. But she *had* given him an out...because they'd gotten too close and it freaked the hell out of him.

Unknowingly, she'd handed him the perfect excuse he was grappling for to keep her safely at a distance. Low blow as it might be, he'd take that pretext and use it. Anything to keep from opening up his life to someone again. Anything to avoid being vulnerable.

Hating himself even as he took the easy way out, he nodded, strongly suspecting her being rejected over the pregnancy would sting to the core. And he hated himself for it. Hated to face how messed up he still was. Hated to impose that on her.

"I'm not looking for a husband, if that's what you're thinking."

"I know that." But hadn't she been disappointed when her ex hadn't offered marriage?

He dared to look into her eyes to see the broken-hearted expression he'd put there and quickly realized he may as well have taken a knife to his own flesh.

Chapter Five

Leif suffered through his attraction to Marta over the next couple of weeks, suspecting she loathed him for rejecting her over the pregnancy. It hurt like hell, but there was no point in pursuing their attraction, so he let her think the worst of him.

He watched her get up each day decked in overalls and a T-shirt and head over to the college to paint the outdoor mural. On the first day, he'd loaded his truck with the supplies and cans of paint, wondering how she'd manage to do the hard labor on her own. Painting to the scale of the walls, one inch to one foot, seemed a daunting task for a lady barely five-feet-six-inches tall.

Once at the college he delivered her supplies and was surprised to find a team organized and waiting to help. Desi Rask, a new enrollee in the art department, had arranged the group, which included Elke Norling, Ben

Cobowa and a handful of other art students. Anything Marta needed, they jumped to the task, making it happen. Honestly, Leif felt a little useless. So after he delivered the combination ladder/scaffold work platform for the higher-up painting, he'd left and hadn't gone back.

To make up for the fruitless feeling, he dived into his private project to find a way to remove what they suspected to be buried treasure from the sacred ground, hoping to do the least amount of damage in the process.

The town was already in an upheaval over the news about their distorted history. There seemed to be two clear factions—those who embraced the pirate story and those who were horrified by it. Personally, it wasn't an issue for him; there was nothing they could do about it so they may as well make the most of the attention it would bring. As the local small business folks said, the influx of tourists would be good for everyone.

The committee knew they couldn't keep the buried treasure a secret much longer. Leif needed to complete and present his report ASAP. As a result, he worked long hours with the engineer consultants reviewing the infrared thermal study findings. What they came up with was the best, nondestructive way to positively identify the trunk and its contents. He knew where to get the equipment to do the job. Removing it with a straight-down dig would only disrupt a tiny fragment of the entire burial grounds. And that was the sticking point. He hoped it would be considered a compromise.

The special committee was divided over his report at the Thursday-night meeting. Ben and Elke were firm on not disrupting the sacred ground for any reason. Even the lure of potentially millions of dollars in ancient coins and jewels, which could benefit the college and the entire town, wouldn't change their minds. Jarl Madsen waffled between the benefit to the Maritime Museum the findings would bring and the principle of respecting the Chinook spirits. The rest of the committee voted to move forward with the plan, and though Leif admitted to being uncomfortable with the task, he felt it was necessary.

Division seemed to be the term of the day and the theme of their meeting, and when Leif arrived home with a pounding headache, the last thing he wanted was to be taunted by Marta. Yet there she stood at the base of the staircase, wearing a silky, long, flowing, cream-colored dress with a wide leather belt that matched her open-toed shoes and a linen bolero jacket that had a collar more suited for a bathrobe. Her hair hung loose over her shoulders, and with large gold hoop earrings, she looked gorgeous as always, even while nailing him with a serious stare.

"How'd the meeting go?" she asked.

"As to be expected. How is the mural coming along?" Maybe he could divert the line of questioning.

She raised a brow as if he'd asked a loaded question or had dodged her question. He should have known the tactic wouldn't get by her.

"The mural's great. We're moving along really well. At this rate I should be out of your hair within another month to six weeks."

Did she really think all he wanted to do was get rid of her? Was that why she'd dressed to slay him with that getup and those red toenails? "That wasn't my point."

"I understand." No she didn't, but he was too tired and wiped out to argue. Though seeing her had instantly revived a basic part of him. "Listen, I overheard Elke and Ben talking about more bad news at school today.

Is that why you've been so busy lately, why you had this meeting tonight?"

He nodded. Why deny it? Everything would come out within a week after the citywide vote because the committee had decided to go public again. "Yep. This pirate business seems to be the gift that just keeps on giving."

With folded arms she stepped closer, and even from this distance, his body reacted to her.

"How so?"

He inhaled and rubbed his jaw. "You mind if I pour myself a drink?"

"Of course not. It's your house." Now she looked downright curious. "What's going on, Leif?"

He strode to the wet bar in the corner of the living room and poured two fingers of Glenlivet Scotch whiskey straight up, swirled the liquid in the glass, took a drink and plopped down on the nearest chair beside the fireplace. If she weren't pregnant, he would have offered her a snifter. The liquor burned its way down his throat, with a welcomed woodsy taste accompanying it. Due to his empty stomach, he almost immediately felt the relaxing effect.

Marta had followed him into the room and primly sat on the edge of the adjacent wing-back chair, catching her hair and putting it all over one shoulder, making her look sexy as hell. She took off her shoes and dug her toes into the fluffy faux-animal-fur rug. Man, she was driving him crazy. Was it intentional?

"So part of our findings from the beginning were these journals. You know the story." She'd read all of the newspaper articles, so he knew she was aware of the facts. "We also found a map made by Captain Prince, and the journal indicated a second trunk, which he'd buried. I hired a company to provide an infrared imaging of the area in question, and the consensus is this alleged second pirate trunk is buried on the wrong side of the Ringmuren."

"Seriously?" Her eyes were wide, and under the recessed ceiling lights they looked the color of his whiskey.

"So once again, we're in the middle of a mess. Do we dig for it or respect the grounds?" A rhetorical question.

"Respect the sacred grounds," she said without blinking.

"It's not that easy."

"Yes, it is."

He shook his head slowly and took another drink, rolled the liquid around in his mouth for the fullest effect, then swallowed. "Nothing is ever that easy."

And that could be the metaphor for his life. Already the drink had worked its wonders, making him go all philosophical as part of the process. For Marta, everything seemed easy-peasy. How different they were.

"Heartlandia could benefit from the treasures in the trunk on more levels than we can count. The citizens will vote on it."

"It would be disrespectful and nothing good would come of it."

"You don't know that."

"I guarantee it."

"How can you be so damn sure of everything?"

She tossed her head. "It's a gift, I guess."

She sounded sarcastic, and Leif suspected things weren't over yet. He decided to put the topic to rest for now by pointing her in another direction. "So any questions you have can get answered at the next town meeting." Yeah, it was a cop-out, but he wanted off the hot seat. Now.

She gave a quick nod but kept watching him.

"Do me a favor and quit staring at me like you're reading my mind," he said. "Because I can guarantee you don't have any idea what I'm thinking right now." *Like how beautiful you are, especially when you're riled up.*

"We can agree to disagree on digging or not for now, but count me as the opposition."

"Yeah, I heard that the first time. Too bad you don't get to vote." His drink seemed to call out to him, yet he couldn't tear his gaze from hers. An energy-fueled moment coursed between them and an all too familiar feeling gathered strength throughout his body.

She blinked, then didn't waste another beat before coming at him again. "I'd like to ask a question on an unrelated topic, though."

"Fine with me." Anything to get off the sacred burial grounds. He'd had enough discussion on that tonight for the rest of the year.

She lowered her eyes and smoothed her skirt, then glanced back up. "I can't quite get a grip on how long you intend to live like a hermit." Her voice was soft when she landed her sucker punch.

This was an angle he hadn't bargained for. Considering the fact she lived under the same roof as him and had already figured things out, the pointed question was worthy of an answer. "I don't—"

"Of course you do. You may as well still be wearing your wedding ring."

Anger flashed through him. She must have seen it in his eyes.

"Forgive me for being indelicate, but I'm just being real."

Was it sympathy he saw in her expression? Damn it, he didn't want to be pitied, so he went stoic and brooded.

"Look," she said. "It's obvious we're attracted to each other, yet when I touch you, you act as if I've thrown acid on you."

Was this why she'd dressed like that and waited for him to come home? To finally have it out? "That's a lie."

"And you're the lousiest liar I've ever met. For the record, I didn't buy that phony excuse about my pregnancy, either."

"You're the one who suggested it."

"A ploy, and you glommed onto it...desperately."

Indeed he had, as if the skies had suddenly opened up and rained down excuses for being a loner, he'd taken her suspicion of his resistance being because of the pregnancy and run with it. "Wait. You didn't believe me?"

"Hell no. But I knew you couldn't go on kissing me. I know you're not able to move on with your life yet, but what I don't understand is why."

With his jaw locked tight, he rolled the last of the whiskey around in his glass, looking at it rather than at Marta's sharp and knowing stare. Then he downed it. How could a guy feel so naked when fully dressed?

"I'm not here forever." Her voice had softened. "In the meantime, we could help each other forget. It could be healing even."

He lifted his eyes to her, sensing a glimmer of hope while feeling the weight of the world on his chest. Her cheeks were flushed, her pupils large. Passion radiated from her, pulsing over him, forging another chink in his quickly dwindling armor.

She wasn't suggesting forever. She was offering now. And it shook his world down to the root.

He was tired of dropping out of his personal life. Sick and tired of wanting but not taking. On instinct, he put down his glass, stood and walked toward Marta. Pulling her up and into his arms, he took control of the moment, drawing her close, fitting his mouth to hers, kissing her as he'd wanted to for days. Like the first time he'd kissed her, she responded to his touch with the passion she'd just hurled at him, along with those challenging words to knock him out of his rut.

She'd done more than that.

Her mouth had already become familiar, and he captured it with the lunge of his tongue. He held her close and tight, aware of her full breasts pressed to his chest, her hips flush to his, the energy that arced between them. He inhaled that crazy cinnamon-spice scent and whatever the hell else it was. Exploring her lips and tongue, the kiss set off threads of heat and longing that laced a twisted path to his groin. Losing control with each kiss, he deepened it, pulled back and dived in again. And again.

Lost in her, his fingers dug into her hair, loving the thickness and satin feel, and keeping her mouth exactly where he wanted it. They breathed each other and made out like randy teenagers, enjoying a clandestine moment outside of time. This wasn't forever, she'd said. That concept had clicked, and for whatever crazy reason, he'd come to a point where he could deal with that. The right now.

Long heady moments passed as they kissed, caressed and explored, his body waking up kiss by kiss from its extended sleep, hungry for more. And more.

Marta bracketed his face with her hands and, revealing her flushed cheeks and swollen lips from his over-enthusiastic kisses, pleaded with her eyes. "We can do this, Leif. It's ours for the taking. Just for now. I promise I don't come with strings."

He fought for focus, his ears ringing, his body zinging with impulses. "You've got to understand something first."

She watched and waited.

"I don't know about healing or right now or being good for each other," he said. "I don't understand any of it. All I know is you make me want to do things I've tried to forget, and you're driving me crazy."

Concern flashed in her eyes. Did it finally compute how hard she pushed his defenses? "We don't have to rush it, then," she said, dropping her hands and edging out of his arms. "As long as we know we're on the same page."

And that was the problem. Was he on the same page as her? An affair? Short and convenient. While they just happened to be living under the same roof. Could he separate emotions from a physical relationship with the snap of a finger? Could he be with someone new after the twelve years he'd devoted to Ellen? Right now it seemed like forever since he'd been with her. Tension crept back into his body.

"It's been a long day," Marta said, her palm skimming the length of his chest, taunting him without effort. "You're welcome to join me in my bed…" Before he could open his mouth she lifted her hand. "Or think about my offer awhile longer." Her serene smile indicated it wasn't a test, that in some way she understood. "No pressure. Honestly. I'm good either way."

Still looking flushed, with her hair messed from his hands, she gave the hint of a smile, turned and left the room with her head held high. After taking the stairs quickly, she disappeared.

Half in shock—he'd never had a woman be so blatant before—Leif drank the last drops in his glass and closed his eyes while it curled down his throat. Then he poured more.

If he needed fortification to make love to a beautiful and vibrant woman like Marta, he still wasn't ready. Sad but true.

But he wanted to be ready; God, he wanted to be. He'd finally admitted it—well, she'd forced him to—but even that was progress.

He finished off his glass, then climbed the stairs, his legs feeling like sandbags yet his mind whirling with desire and possibilities. At the top he glanced toward Marta's room, his old bedroom. The final stumbling block between them. The thought of making love to her in there, where he and Ellen had shared the bed, mixed him up beyond belief. When he took her—and after her come-on just now he would, he was sure of that—it would be in *his* bed, in *his* room, under *his* conditions.

Taking Marta up on one more of her offers—to think things over—he turned right instead of left and headed for the smaller guest room, his room. It was definitely time to quit being a guest in his own house; Marta's suggestion had made that clear. His father used to say a man needed to be the king of his castle. Damn right.

Whoever this woman was, pregnant or not, he wanted her...just for now. She'd promised, no strings. He could deal with that.

That night, surprisingly, he went right to sleep, and

whether or not fueled by whiskey, Ellen came to him in his dream. Healthy Ellen, not his wife from their last months together. She looked so real he wanted to touch her, but she stayed beyond his reach. Her beautiful smile nearly made him cry. *Stop it*, he could have sworn he heard her say. *Quit waiting*. Her form drifted closer, her face near enough to kiss, but he couldn't make his head or hands move to touch her. Without uttering a sound she communicated with him. *Live your life. I'm the one who died, not you*. And then, long before he was ready to lose her again, she was gone.

Leif woke up, raising to his elbows, searching the room as if expecting to find her hiding in the corners. His heart raced. Ellen. God he missed her.

Slowly the words she'd said in the dream repeated in his mind. *Stop it. Quit waiting. Live your life. I'm the one who died, not you.*

He lay back on his pillow and rubbed his forehead. Had she released him? He pinched his temples and thought. Or, after three years had he finally released himself? He'd mourned her long and with all of his heart. It was okay to move on, the dream seemed to say. Wasn't that what Marta had said, too?

He got out of bed and paced his room. The large fan-light window above the French doors let in a trickle of moonlight, intensifying the shadows. He was alive and Ellen was gone, yet he'd been living like a dead man, a ghost. Opening his house to Marta and her persistence had finally forced him to face it.

He thought about the lady down the hall, so open and willing to share her affections, and how he'd shut her down. He hoped he hadn't lost the chance to show her that blood actually ran through his veins. Tomorrow was another day, and it was filled with possibilities. Hell, what about tonight? Right now? The thought drilled a path right to his gut and put a smile on his face. He could carry her to his room and make love to her under the moonlight until morning.

Heading for the bathroom to freshen up he heard loud moans quickly followed by a sharp, pain-filled groan.

"Leif!" Marta called out, and he sprinted toward her room.

Chapter Six

Marta tossed and turned in bed with discomfort. The ache had started an hour ago, and it suddenly had escalated. At first she'd thought it was an emotional response to taking that risk with Leif and putting herself on the line. Again.

The offer had drummed up memories of old arguments with her mother, too. How they'd fought over Marta's carefree ways with men. Gabriella had tried every trick in the book to restrain her daughter, but that had only made Marta more determined to prove she didn't need traditional marriage or commitment with men.

The joke had been on her, though, because Lawrence had let her down. She'd promised to be a woman without strings when they'd started dating. He'd been married once already, with young-adult children ready to fly the nest; the last thing he wanted was another marriage...

another child. She'd said she was fine with that. He'd offered travel, parties, hobnobbing with the important people in the art world. Everything a young artist could hope for. He'd given her all of that, then spoiled her by supporting her and her art.

Her mother had accused her of being a kept woman, but Marta made excuses. *No. He's my benefactor. He believes in my talent.*

He pays your rent and you give him sex, her mother had shot back. Insulted by what she'd insinuated, Marta stormed out.

They'd never ironed out their differences, had never said they were sorry, and Marta hadn't spoken to her mother the last year of her life. Now she was dead. And Marta was pregnant. Lawrence didn't want to marry her. And she'd just offered Leif a "no strings" fling.

Would she ever learn?

Would she ever honor her mother's biggest wish for her?

The answer hurt. God, it hurt to remember.

The pain in her gut never settled down, either.

Now a sharp pang cut through her side, making her cry out.

"Leif!"

Within seconds he came rushing into the room, flipping on the light, looking mortified. "What's wrong?"

"I'm not sure." She squinted at him through the harsh light.

"Where do you hurt?"

"Here." She uncurled her body and moved her hand around her lower abdomen.

His eyes went wide, and a shocked and concerned expression covered his face. "You need a doctor." He rushed to the phone beside her bed and punched in some numbers. Having never been pregnant before, and to be honest, unnerved by the intensity of her pain, she didn't protest.

"Kent? Sorry to call so late, but it's Marta. She's doubled over in pain, and honestly, I'm worried for the baby." He pinched the bridge of his nose, closed his eyes and listened. "Thank you!"

Leif hung up, immediately returned to Marta's side and took her hand. "He's on his way over."

Though Sedona had many small-town qualities, this selfless attitude seemed unique to Heartlandia. Did doctors even make house calls anymore? Evidently they did here.

Having Leif beside her helped settle the nerves coiling through her. He'd verbalized her greatest fear—he was worried for the baby. So was she. She was just getting used to the life-changing circumstances, but she'd embraced the thought of becoming a mother. Wanted to be a good mother like hers had been.

And the craziest part of all was, she wanted to go about it the same way her mother did, even if the cart had gotten before the horse.

Was this a cruel joke from the universe? Dangling motherhood before her. Forcing her to admit she wanted a more traditional life, including marriage, only to yank it away from her?

As if reading her mind, he gathered her close and held tight. "What can I do for you?"

"Just hold me." She snuggled in, feeling curiously safe and secure through the waves of pain.

He gently rocked her, helping the gripping to back off

a little. Then he kissed the top of her head. This from the hermit? Even in pain, she felt his tenderness.

Earlier she'd been stunned when Leif had admitted he hadn't backed away from her because of the pregnancy. She'd fibbed about knowing otherwise, recalling how deeply his candid confession had struck that day at his mother's memorial bench. But she'd held out, thinking the best thoughts, that he'd come around, see the light. Negativity wasn't her style.

Knowing his honest feelings—that the pregnancy wasn't an issue for him—renewed her hope. He was a good, solid man worth knowing. Loving even? Who knew? Their circumstances were anything but ideal, and that worried her, but nevertheless, she'd only offered him "just for now." What man in his right mind wouldn't accept?

In her world, that was the only way to truly get to know a man. Turns out old habits die hard. *Sorry, Momma. I'm a work in progress.*

Not more than fifteen minutes later the doorbell rang, rousing the dogs who'd been hovering around the bed since sensing something was wrong.

"It's okay," Leif said to quiet them as he took off down the stairs.

Marta immediately missed his warmth and the comfort he gave. Even though she still hurt, his being there had made it bearable. Another wave of cramping built, and she curled back into a ball.

Heavy footsteps soon ascended the stairs and Marta came face to face with Desi's fiancé. Desi had said he looked like a Viking, and she hadn't been lying. She'd even shown Marta a picture on the cell phone, but it hadn't done him justice. Well over six feet tall with a build to match, the big man had nothing but concern on his kind face.

He reached out to take her hand. "I'm Kent Larson. So tell me what's going on."

Leif left the room as the good doctor began his examination. He couldn't help but recall the many times Kent had come to the house during Ellen's final months. Remembering the pain and suffering she'd gone through made his skin crawl. How he'd felt helpless and angry and wished he could be the one dying, not his wife. God, he couldn't go through these memories right now.

How could he ever let himself care that much for anyone again? And if he couldn't ever care that much for anyone, it wouldn't be fair to get involved. That had been his mantra for the past three years. But earlier Marta had offered "just for now" and it had thrown him sideways. How could he even think these thoughts now? The woman was in pain. Possibly losing her baby. Now wasn't the time to think about anything but her well-being.

Damn it. Where Marta was concerned, he already *was* in over his head.

He tried to talk himself down from the growing panic of the caring-losing cycle. This was a completely different situation from his wife's. Marta was not dying from cancer. From his personal experience, he'd probably always overreact in situations like these. He worried about the baby and whether Marta would need to be admitted to the nearest hospital forty miles away. Would they need to call an ambulance? The memory of an ambulance coming to his door, taking his wife away, never to return home again, sent a shiver down his spine. Damn. Damn. Damn it all.

He paced outside the room, then went to the kitchen and made himself a cup of herbal tea—the kind Marta had been drinking for weeks now, the kind that was supposed to have a calming effect—and paced some more.

A few minutes later, he stared out the kitchen's dark window but only saw his reflection in the glass. That freaked-out expression made him flinch as memory after memory haunted his thoughts. No, he couldn't let himself be in that situation ever again.

Kent called his name from the top of the staircase.

"Yo! I'm coming." He rushed up the stairs and took his first deep breath when he saw the relaxed expression on Kent's face.

"What we have here is a pregnant lady taken out by the current intestinal flu. I've seen no less than a dozen patients in the past two days with the exact same symptoms."

"The baby's okay?"

He nodded. "Did a thorough examination and everything checks out. The bad news is, there's no shortcut or treatment for this flu. It'll have to run its course for the next two to three days. The intestinal pain should subside within twelve hours, with lingering digestive symptoms after that. You know the drill. Keep her hydrated and call me if anything unusual develops."

Leif slapped Kent's shoulder. "Thank you, man. What do I owe you?"

"Your crew just painted my house for barely the price of the cans of paint. I say we're even."

No point in arguing.

"Thanks." That was how the community had always worked, each person helping the other, and it went all the way back to the fisherman and native Chinook, just like the town monument depicted.

"Any time."

Their respect being mutual, the men walked in silence down the stairs as Leif showed Kent out.

Immediately back on task, Leif rushed the stairs and found Marta asleep, her face occasionally grimacing but otherwise looking peaceful. Rather than go back to bed, he turned the dimmer to night-light level, sat in the bedside chair and rested his shoeless feet on the corner of the mattress.

"Thank you," she whispered.

He grasped around in the shadows, found her forearm and squeezed. "You're welcome."

Over the next couple of days Leif saw the worst of Marta, which wasn't bad at all, and the best of himself. He'd stood guard outside the bathroom door whenever she'd made a mad dash or while she cleaned up. He'd fed her when she was too weak to lift her soup bowl. He'd memorized every freckle on her face and the thickness of her eyelashes when she slept, and he'd learned how to braid her hair. He'd been through this drill before, knew how to care for a sick woman—a dying woman.

But Marta wasn't dying. She was very much alive, and every day she looked and felt better, and that made all the difference in his attitude.

"I can't stand another day without a shower," she said on Sunday, day three.

"Let's do it."

"Let's?" She cast a questionable glance, sitting at the bedside, gingerly lowering her feet to the floor.

Caring for her had given him a false sense of inti-

macy, but she'd cleared that right up. "I'll be nearby if
you need me," he said.

She tried to stand but her knees went wobbly. "Maybe
I better take a bath instead."

"I'll run the water. Wait here."

Back in a jiffy, the bath filling with warm water, he as-
sisted her into the bathroom. Wearing loose pajamas covered in cartoon owls, she sat on the edge of the extralarge
soaking tub and smiled. He'd even lit some scented candles to help her relax.

She gazed up coyly. "You can go now."

He lifted one corner of his mouth in a smile. "If you
say so."

She tossed a "seriously?" glance. "I say so."

With his smile stretching into a full-blown grin, Leif
turned and left but hovered nearby, changing the sheets
on her bed while she bathed.

"Leif?" she called out after several minutes. "I need
to wash my hair. Can you bring my shampoo?"

He finished plumping the pillow and went to the bathroom door. "Knock, knock. Is it in there?"

"Yes, in the shower."

To be polite he covered his eyes and walked past the
tub toward the sink and on toward the shower stall, feeling his way along the walls. She laughed. "I'm covered."

Disappointed, he looked, hoping she really wasn't,
but found she'd added bubbles to the tub and had put the
washcloth across her chest. A beautiful sight, her hair
piled high on her head and her dark eyes striking the
perfect balance of bashful yet sexy.

"I'm a great hair washer," he said, sadness striking
like an electric jolt with the quick memory of the two

of them in the tub washing his wife's hair before it had started falling out.

Marta picked up on the brief mood change, but instead of letting the moment pass, she surprised him. "I could use your help."

He knelt beside the tub and turned on the water, letting it trickle over his fingers until it warmed. She turned away from him and sat, shifting through the water so her head was closer to the handheld shower sprayer, affording him a glance at her back. She stayed sitting with her back to him, and he ran the water over her hair. After adding shampoo he lathered it up, careful not to get soap in her eyes, loving the feel of his fingers entangled in the suds and hair. She arched her neck, and he rinsed, glancing over her shoulder and taking in all her femininity, down to the curve of her throat and the top of her breasts. Through the waning bubbles he could see the heart-shaped swell of her hips and bottom where she sat, the intimacy nearly undoing him.

When he was done he wrapped her hair snugly in a towel, handed her a second bath towel, activated the drain and left her to dry in privacy. Walking out the door while wanting to see her standing and fully naked proved to be one of the hardest things he'd done in the past three years.

He wanted her, and things would never be the same between them.

Seeing her, touching her, caring for her had cracked through the last of his armor, gripping his heart and forcing him to feel again. Closing the bathroom door, Leif realized there was no going back, and he was incapable of doing "just for now." He was crazy about Marta, wanted only the best for her, and if she was just looking for a fling, he had a big surprise for her.

* * *

By the fourth day, Monday, Marta felt 90 percent better physically, but one thought plagued her conscience. She'd become completely dependent on Leif—he housed her, fed her, even took care of her when she was sick— and she'd promised she'd never be in that position again. She'd learned the hard way with Lawrence. Yet she felt grateful for everything Leif had done for her during her bout with the flu. She cringed thinking there was almost nothing she could hide from him now.

What a crazy relationship they'd forged in seven short weeks.

In her postflu weakness, she worried about jumping from one failed relationship into another superficial one. From one rich and powerful man to another…one who also signed her paycheck. Leif had made it quite clear that the city council couldn't afford her, and he'd stepped in to get the mural painted. It was a legacy he wanted to leave for his family as well as himself, she knew it. In this regard, he was just as much her benefactor as Lawrence had been.

Hell, before she'd gotten sick, in that moment of nearly unbearable sexual desire, she'd invited Leif into her bed. Did she want to repeat the pattern with him, or break that promise of independence?

Yet she'd been the one to suggest they help each other heal, and at the time she'd meant every word. She missed the closeness of making love with a man, believed it would be good for her and the baby, too. The truth was hard to take, and lying in bed for days had forced her to think through things. Being near Leif, the different way he made her feel, honored and cherished even, she'd realized the spark had died between her and Lawrence long before she'd gotten pregnant. What could she expect from accepting his offer—just you and me and the world of art? His underwhelming response when she'd told him about the baby had dashed out the final embers. There was no room in his life or heart for a child. Which meant there was no longer room for Marta, either.

Seeing Leif at his best, an open, giving and tender man, had sharpened the contrast. As she looked back with a clear eye, she could see Lawrence had maintained a cushion of distance for five years and had subtly made it known who had the power. As far as she was concerned the only thing the men had in common was the first letter of their names.

As her strength returned, so did her resolve to think of Leif as a transition. He was her now, not her future. She could and would deal with that. Besides, she couldn't expect any man to accept another man's baby before it was even born, could she? Hell, the baby's own father couldn't. Leif said he did, after saying he didn't. That left just enough doubt to keep her guessing. And she couldn't live or think like that anymore. She had a bigger job to do—being a future mother.

No, she and Leif would have whatever they had while she was here, and that would be it. She couldn't hope for more, even though, when she was completely honest, she did want more than that. *I get it now, Momma. Okay?* But when? And with who?

Ack, maybe she'd take just this one last day to rest and straighten out her thoughts. Because from where she lay, everything that had seemed so logical and sophisticated before she'd gotten ill—just for now—was suddenly a jumbled-up mess and a gamble with her heart she wasn't sure she could or should take.

Leif had stayed home from work on her account, so at the end of the day she put on her long, flowing lounge dress, the same one she'd worn the other night. She noticed she'd lost a little weight, so she tightened the belt around her waist. Before she left her room, she threw on a golden-threaded slate-colored shawl and some gold sandals and headed downstairs for her first dinner out of bed in days.

"Something smells fantastic," she said, entering the kitchen.

Leif turned his head while stirring a pot of bubbling water. "Someone *looks* fantastic, too. You'd never know you'd been sick."

"You lie, but thank you anyway."

"You don't believe me? Come here."

She stepped closer and he put his hand on her waist, pulled her near, looked her straight in the eyes with a mischievous gaze and kissed her. Wrapping her arms around his neck, returning his affection, she marveled over this changed man and how natural they felt together. Even knowing him for such a short time, she felt completely comfortable in his embrace. As if they belonged together. With all the confidence in the world he kissed her lips, her neck, took her hair into his hand and lightly tugged on it. When the kiss ended, he made a soft sound in his throat; she was covered with tingly bumps and he had fire in his eyes. And her resolve about "just for now" had definitely melted into "maybe something more."

The boiling water frothed and splashed over the top of the pot, taking his immediate attention. With a wooden spoon he fished out one piece of corkscrew-shaped pasta, blew on it, then tossed it into his mouth, eyes wide from the heat.

Blowing out while chewing, he grinned. "Al dente. Perfect."

Her hands flew to her mouth in a prayer pose while she lightly laughed. Such a silly and fun man, not afraid to be himself for fear of coming off uncool or out of control...unlike Lawrence.

"You like beef stroganoff?"

"Love it."

"You and the baby need the protein, and you can use the calories. Want to grab those rolls for me?"

She followed his orders and put the basket of bread on the already set table while he dished out the noodles and covered them with stroganoff sauce. Her mouth watered—another positive sign the curse of the flu had passed.

With Marta and Leif both being ravenous, dinner became a series of contented sounds and food-lover faces, plus occasional glances that imparted so much more. Two people who knew how to enjoy food. Could it be a metaphor for enjoying sex together? They'd definitely reached a new level of closeness since she'd had the nerve to invite him into her bed, and it was obvious he wanted to take her up on it—though he'd chickened out originally. Then she'd gotten ill and had allowed Leif to care for her, and she couldn't run or hide from him. Only one thing more was needed between them: complete intimacy. She'd felt bold and worldly when she'd called Leif a hermit and dangled the carrot of making love before him. Now? Considering everything they'd built between them, like friendship and trust, making love with Leif would change that, and that bold and worldly part...she wasn't feeling so much anymore.

When dinner was finished, together they carried the

dishes to the sink. As she turned on the water to rinse them, his hand joined hers under the stream, testing the temperature. As their fingers touched, her temperature definitely went up.

"I'll get this," he said.

"I want to help."

He reached behind, then handed her a towel, gently drying her fingers first. Their gazes connected for a second and a tiny bubble of adrenaline popped in her chest. "You can dry."

She stood too close when he turned to hand her the first plate and their shoulders bumped. "Oh, excuse me," she said.

He gave a quick peck to her cheek. "I forgive you, but what for?"

His ice-blue eyes melted any doubt she'd allowed to build up tonight. And if her sudden willingness to be with him wasn't proof enough, her charging pulse was the final clue.

She found the only remaining forks on the counter and put them into the sudsy water, his hand quickly finding hers in the water, running his thumb over her knuckles. "So how are you feeling?"

Pretty damn fine. He obviously waited for a sign, and here was the kicker—Ms. Bold and Modern suddenly felt nervous. Leif wasn't like any man she'd been with before. He didn't play games or need to prove anything or flaunt his position of power. Wasn't he the richest man in Heartlandia? Couldn't prove it by her.

His strength, character and sense of permanence rattled her to the core.

"I'm all better." Her voice sounded softer than usual,

tentative even. What was coming over her? *Momma, don't mess with me now. Please.*

To distract herself from the odd insecure reaction, she got busy opening a cupboard, ready to put some dishes away, but he stopped her. She shifted her glance to his. He shook his head. *Not now.* Then he dried his hands and turned off the water, took her by the palm and led her toward the stairs.

Mute, she followed, out-of-the-blue jitters budding in her center. Where had her worldly woman confidence gone? The thought of being with Leif had made her blood run hot, yet now the reality of it threw her off balance. Theirs could never be a fling, and that was all she'd been used to with men. What would it be like to find that "once in a lifetime" love her father always talked about? Her head spun with the thoughts as Leif guided her toward the stairs.

Was she ready to throw away this chance to know Leif in the truest sense because of imperfect circumstances?

Chip and Dale eagerly romped up the steps with them but Leif sent the dogs away. Obeying their master, sensing he had something planned that didn't involve them, the dogs lowered their heads and tromped off to their downstairs beds.

When Leif and Marta reached the top of the stairs, his hand tugging her to the right instead of left, she let doubt creep back in full force. Leif was completely different from the man who'd let her down, but the current situation of being dependent on him rang too familiar. Though she'd agreed to a business arrangement, it smacked of power and dependence, one over the other, a subtle but steady struggle that she couldn't quite get a grip on. The circumstances were too similar; she was supposed to learn from her mistakes. She stopped.

"Maybe this isn't such a good idea after all," she said, nowhere near convincing herself, yet edging her hand from his until only their fingertips touched.

He looked at her with a probing gaze, as if asking, "Now who is afraid?" Then, calling her out, he gave the most confident smile she'd ever seen.

"Like hell it isn't," he said, sweeping her up and carrying her toward his bedroom.

Chapter Seven

Marta sank into Leif's powerful arms as he carried her to the bedroom. He used his foot to open the door and she soon realized he'd planned this seduction well in advance. The fragrance of musk disguised in sandal-wood from scented candles permeated the atmosphere of the room, which looked damned sexy with the turned-down covers and shiny sheets. The bed faced French doors covered only by sheers. Dusk provided enough light to see his face, rugged and craggy from hard outdoor labor and sexy, so, so sexy. His was the face that had quickly become her measure for handsomeness against all other men.

Tingling sensations began coiling through the soles of her feet to the insides of her thighs and upward. Her breath slipped out of sync as she gazed up at Leif and anticipated making love with him for the first time.

He dropped her feet lightly to the floor, pulled her close and, holding her face, kissed her gently, arousing a stronger reaction than any hot, wet and wild kiss would. His timing was perfect. Start slow, build from there, though she sensed his overwhelming struggle to contain himself. It taunted and energized her and, because her hands were free, she began fumbling and thrashing away at the buttons on his shirt.

The kisses deepened, their sounds luscious and hungry, nearly torturing her. The deep coiling throughout her body turned warm and itchy as she matched his probing tongue. Woozy from the heightening need, she held on to the shirt fabric as his hands gripped her shoulders, then skimmed her upper body, feeling her every curve, releasing chills along her skin. She stripped him of his shirt and ran her palms over his muscular chest and flat stomach. The feel of his skin, surprisingly smooth, nearly sent sparks up her arms.

Obviously wanting her naked, he pulled the skirt of her dress all the way from the floor to over her head in record time. That left her glad she'd worn her favorite lacy peach-colored underwear, though the small baby bump made her feel a twinge of self-consciousness.

His urgent gaze scanned her head to toe but soon settled on her chest, passion and longing so obvious any insecurity disappeared and her nipples pebbled beneath the lace. Had she ever felt so needed before? She stepped forward and he unlatched the front clasp of the bra, the weight of her breasts released and free to the cool evening air. With his face expressing amazement and desire, first one hand explored her tender skin, then the other, lifting, caressing, lightly passing a thumb over the sensitive tips. A faint admiring curse escaped his lips. He bent forward and kissed first one then the other breast, inhaling her scent while the beauty of his touch rolled through her. Cradling his head, she kissed the crown of his hair, surprised by the softness, then leaned forward and nuzzled his ear and neck, his shower-fresh scent similar to the candles. On a deep inhale he rose and pulled her close to his chest, flesh to flesh, heat fanning from every point of contact, his mouth devouring her neck, earlobe and jaw. Then, placing a palm on each of her hips, in a hungry move he pulled her closer, and she found the strong erection beneath his jeans. Nothing short of electricity arced between them as they caressed and explored each other.

He lifted her again and placed her on the cold, silky sheets. On her elbow, she waited to welcome him as he dived next to her.

"Hold on," she said, unzipping his jeans.

He flashed a quick look of chagrin, then gladly let her do the honor. The man's neon green underwear both surprised and delighted her when she got on her knees and pulled the jeans off from the leg cuffs. The boxer briefs fit snug over those thickly muscled thighs and outlined his erection. The sight of him crashing through her.

Her breath caught. *So gorgeous.* How could he live like a hermit when women probably had been beating down his door? He didn't give her near enough time to enjoy the view as he tugged her up by the waist and lightly tossed her onto her back. She laughed, then got serious, watching as the urgency shifted gears while he removed her lacy thong as though unwrapping a delicate package. Then, much quicker, he removed his own underwear, freeing that full erection. The vision branded her brain. She wanted him. Without a doubt.

She reached for his thighs, ran her hand along the powerful muscles and took him into her grip, skimming the silky skin over solid strength, her thumb pressing over the head.

Would she ever forget this moment?

Then all her thoughts left as he shifted and took her into his arms. Starting at her head and mouth, then covering all points south, he fought his own need, solely concentrating on her, thoroughly and desperately making love to her body. Wanting nothing more than to please her.

Her breath ragged, her skin burning with desire long before he was finished showing her how he needed her, she bucked beneath him, ready, so, so ready for him. Snapping out of his enthralled sexual haze, he got down to the business of sheathing himself from the tiny package he'd removed from his bedside drawer. Quickly back on task, little by little he entered her, and more quiet oaths and prayers tumbled out of his lips.

Soon molding to each other, closer than seemed humanly possible, they rocked together, finding the rhythm that was exclusively theirs. Discovering what worked and what drove the other crazy. Marta felt as starved for this moment as Leif must have been, as she followed his demanding pace, nearly burning up the sheets beneath her one moment, then slowing to draw out the exquisite pleasure the next.

Rolling on top, she took control, loving the sublime expression on his face when she did. His verbal outbursts as she frantically made love to him prodded her on. She wanted to drive him wild and, from the tense muscles and desperate expression on his face, she was. Every nerve ending in her body vibrated with the energy buzzing through her because of him.

His jaw clenched and he grabbed her hips, holding her firm against him as he, amazingly, increased the speed, spiraling the tension, whisking her to the edge of release and dangling her there. Her elbows gave out, landing her face to his neck, and she tasted the salt of the sweat they'd worked up together. Willing herself back up, gasping for air, she bucked on top as he pounded into her and kept her suspended so close to heaven she could barely breathe. After what seemed like blissful eternity, he set off an implosion at her center so intense, she moaned and cried out and, unable to hold herself up another second, she collapsed onto his chest again. The orgasm rolled through every cell in her body, drenching her. He rode out the waves of her release, extending them on and on, and only when she'd finished, he finally let himself come.

Several seconds later, still breathing rough and ragged, she could hardly get the words out. "You're amazing."

He panted, too. "We're amazing."

Now realizing what she would have missed if she'd let her better judgment take over, she thanked whatever wisdom had stopped her from backing out of making love with him. Grateful Leif hadn't let her. He was a sexual force to be reckoned with, a man who had a lot of lost time to make up for, and she was the exceptionally lucky woman he wanted to be with.

For now.

The citywide vote had taken place on Wednesday and today, Friday, the results were going to be revealed. The meeting was set for 10:00 a.m. at the college auditorium. Leif swung by the mural to pick up Marta on his way over.

He hadn't seen the mural in a couple of weeks since they'd steered clear of each other for part of it, then he'd gotten super busy with new projects after that. But each day he arrived home eager to see her, and from the usual welcome he got, the feeling was mutual.

"Wow, you're really clipping along, aren't you?" He squinted, the autumn sun bright and assaulting, yet the vivid colors on the college wall stood out, one lively scene transitioning into another. He spotted a perfect rendition of the Ringmuren and a growing city in the distance in her latest panel, and the Heritage Hotel and the town monument sketched out in the next. She had to be halfway through already. His chest tightened at the prospect of what that meant.

From atop a ladder, Marta put the finishing touch on one of the pine trees in the forest on Hjartalanda Peak. "Hi!" She turned, removed her painting respirator mask, her face beaming. "Yeah, so what do you think?"

"It looks fantastic." And so did she. Even in overalls and a plain white T-shirt, both splattered with paint, with her hair pulled back and covered in a large scarf and not wearing a stitch of makeup, she looked fantastic. Even wearing that mask she looked great. The woman who'd been keeping him and his bed warm for the past week had quickly become the object of his undivided attention. Sometimes when his guard was down, like right now, the thought squeezed the breath out of him. And it reminded him of how he'd first felt about Ellen when she'd finally started dating him. "I didn't realize how fast you painted."

"Preplanning does that for you. Plus I've had a lot of

help from Desi and the crew. All I have to worry about is painting my scenes since they take care of everything else. It's been great."

He glanced down the wall to the two students applying the protective varnish to the finished sections. The viselike pressure around his chest tightened. Everything was moving too fast.

Could she read the caution in his expression? To avoid her scrutiny, he smiled harder than necessary. "Fantastic." He seemed to be stuck on the word.

She cleaned her hands and took off the scarf. "Time for the meeting?"

He nodded. They'd avoided the topic since their argument the night she'd gotten sick. She probably assumed they were still on opposite sides, but the funny thing was, he'd had a change of heart. The debate with Marta had pointed it out and removed the importance of buried treasure in favor of laying the past to rest, leaving the spirits alone and moving the town forward.

"I've got a crew coming to help this afternoon, so I'll just leave things as they are." She approached, and without a second thought, he kissed her. "Mmm," she said.

Something as simple as that buoyed his mood right up to the cumulus clouds dotting the otherwise-clear blue sky and helped him forget the magnitude of the meeting they were about to attend.

As they approached the auditorium, the crowd thickened and the noise level rose. Conversations buzzed across the colorful sea of people as Leif and Marta walked down the aisle toward the stage. Lilly and Desi sat in the second row and had saved a seat for Marta. Leif guided her toward them with his hand at the small of her back. Lilly looked up and smiled at them, her gaze dropping to his hand and quickly toward Desi's eyes. Maybe it was the flush on Marta's cheeks or that sparkle when she gazed at him, but the ladies' quick interchange proved they'd noticed. He thought he saw Lilly mouthing, "What'd I tell you?" to Desi, who then cast a knowing smile first at Leif and another toward Marta.

What was with the lady radar? Or was it all his imagination? To put any questions about their relationship to rest, just before Marta stepped into the row of chairs, he reached for her neck, pulled her close and kissed her. The usual electricity flashed in her eyes afterward, and it made him smile from his heart. As Marta edged her way toward the empty seat, Leif engaged first Lilly then Desi's attention, nodded and hinted at another smile before heading to the stage. *That's right, girls, we're an item.* Oh, to be a fly on that auditorium-chair arm for their conversation.

Gerda had dressed like a mayor today in a navy blue suit with a white blouse, offset by a red, white and blue scarf. Her white hair was swept up into a looser knot than usual, and the word *dignified* immediately came to mind. He'd noticed since Desi had come home Gerda had become more stylish, and it probably had to do with her granddaughter's input. He also noticed how Gerda had stepped up to the tough task of taking on the job of mayor, even with this big mess she'd walked into, and she'd earned his true respect for that.

Leif took his seat next to Gunnar. Gunnar's sister, Elke, sat on the other side, and next to her was Ben Cobowa, who looked grim faced. Leif knew exactly where Ben stood on the topic.

Gerda cleared her throat and spoke into the microphone. "I'd like to call this meeting to order. Please take your seats and quiet down."

Surprisingly, the audience quickly responded with muttering and whispers fading to quiet without having to be asked twice. It proved to Leif how important the citizens of Heartlandia took this vote.

Watching from the podium, it became apparent to Leif that there were distinct groups. The Chinook citizens in one section, college students in another, business owners and restaurateurs congregated in a group and the Scandinavian matriarchs and patriarchs assembled in still another section. He cleared his throat as tension gathered there. Today's meeting might turn to chaos regardless of the outcome of the democratic vote. Making sure he could get to Marta and out the nearest door, if necessary, he listened as Gerda concluded her brief but perfectly worded speech. No one had known the vote tally before her speech.

"The vote was very close, but there was a clear majority. Without further ado, Heartlandia has voted and we have listened. Though we won't rush ahead with anything, we will move forward with the plans to explore and possibly dig up the buried trunk, with the intent of disturbing as little burial ground as completely necessary. This technique will soon be explained in the *Heartlandia Herald*."

Leif glanced at Elke and Ben, alarm tightening their eyes.

Cheers and protests erupted; grumbling and excitement all mixed together in a clamorous stew. Certain brows knitted with distress, concern registered on other faces, victory lit up some eyes and gravity darkened features in others. What a mess.

Gerda used a gavel to bang on the podium, but it didn't do any good. Sgt. Norling stepped up, making three harsh claps in front of the microphone, but to no avail. He whistled through his teeth, renting the air. That got some to quiet down, but others still huddled in heated conversations.

A gentleman who looked as if he'd stepped straight off a movie set walked toward the stage. Clearly Native American, he wore a dark suit with a leather bolo tie, expensive-looking boots and enough turquoise jewelry to open his own Southwest attire store. His hair was long and braided in historical Native American fashion. His stern expression promised further discussion on the supposedly closed topic.

Hadn't they already been through this part? The vote had been cast. In his heart, Leif hoped they'd just drop the whole thing. Forget the trunk had ever been mentioned in the captain's journal and move on, but it was too late. Definitely. And he'd been the one to bring the original trunk to the attention of the powers that be. Regret at seeing his town torn apart made him wish he'd never come forward with his findings, but in his heart he knew it was what he'd had to do.

Lilly had set up an interview with Leif for next week regardless of what the outcome would be. Now, with the vote being final, he planned to explain how he intended to identify the trunk and what was inside without actually digging a huge hole. He'd given this possibility a lot of thought. Maybe if the folks understood the technique they'd calm down.

The visitor spoke to Gerda, and afterward she solemnly glanced at Ben and Elke, who were nearby, then she nodded. He stepped toward the microphone. "My name is William Maquinna. I am a lawyer and am here on behalf of the Chinookan peoples of the Clatsop tribe, who wish to maintain the sanctity of their forefathers' burial ground."

"We took a vote, fair and square." One man, three-quarters back in the auditorium, stood and shouted him down, causing good Scandinavian manners to intervene with an outburst of shushing.

The speaker ignored the man. "We maintain this sacred ground is not in Heartlandia's jurisdiction."

"Mr. Maquinna?" Mayor Rask spoke up tentatively. She leaned toward the mic. "We've done our research, and though the Ringmuren delineates the park from the burial grounds, the land does, in fact, also belong to Heartlandia. I'll be glad to share the maps with you." She glanced up at the audience. "Or anyone."

With the speakers at a standoff, the audience got noisy again, and Gunnar called in the nearby increased police presence. There had never been a riot in Heartlandia, and today wouldn't be any different. It wasn't in their genes. But because emotions were running high, having additional police made sense.

Gunnar got a call and, assessing the brewing situation before him, took it. He spoke less than thirty seconds, while Gerda regained the attention of the audience.

"The town monument's been vandalized," he said to Leif as soon as he hung up. "Someone's sprayed paint all over it."

What if Marta's mural got defaced, too? Leif stood, walked off the stage and strode directly to her. "You need to know something," he said, reaching across the first row to get her hand as the crowd continued on in the unruly fashion.

Hustling to get into the aisle, she followed him to the side of the stage. "What's up?"

"Someone's defaced your grandfather's monument."

Anger sparked in her gaze, and her chin shot up with indignation. "Who would do such a thing?"

"Who knows?"

"I've got to make sure no one ruins my work, too. Let's go," she said.

Like a lioness protecting her young, Marta grabbed Leif's hand and led him toward the door at the side of the stage. He didn't protest, though he glanced back at the auditorium, wondering how things would turn out.

"I knew nothing good would come of this buried-treasure business," she muttered as they pushed through the door.

At least she hadn't said *I told you so.*

"Was my grandfather's work ruined?" she asked as they jog walked toward the history quad.

"Gunnar said they'd used spray paint. The sculpture is granite, right?"

She nodded. "I think we'd better bring in some experts for this job."

"Know anyone?"

"I'll ask around."

When they arrived at the half-painted mural, relief rolled over Leif's nerves and across Marta's face. It was just as they'd left it.

Chapter Eight

Over the weekend, Sgt. Norling caught the misguided college students who'd defaced public property. They'd left a note at the scene stating that all history of Heartlandia was bogus. Thanks to Marta's input, Gunnar had called in the National Park Service experts on graffiti removal. The granite sculpture would require a special restorative cleaning agent for porous stone surfaces, applied with natural bristle brushes. Then, to prevent further damage, the cleanser would be removed with potable water using fan-tipped garden hoses.

Just what Heartlandia needed, another town project focusing on their shaky beginnings.

To keep Marta's project safe, Leif built a sliding protective barrier for the entire length of the mural that could be rolled closed and locked each day. His goal was to give Marta peace of mind. Depending on the state of the city once the mural was completed, the college could elect to leave the weatherproof cover in place or take it down.

Grumbling and heated debates continued all over town during the weekend, and the police had to step up their watch, but no fights had been reported. The biggest protestors were the college students, who'd held a peaceful sit-in at the Ringmuren to make their point.

Monday morning before heading to the mural site, Marta read Lilly's article about Friday's meeting, the outcome and the citywide reaction. The *Herald* reporting was evenhanded. The reader couldn't possibly tell whose side she was on, even though Marta knew personally that Lilly was against any intervention on sacred soil. Lilly ended her weekly column asking the question: "Did the students make a good point, even though choosing the stupid method of vandalism to make it? Or is it possible for a couple of new pieces of information—Captain Prince discovering Heartlandia and potential buried treasure in sacred land—to change everything else this town has been built on?"

Now, as Marta painted the college wall, she considered the article. She expected that in the heat of everything going on, there would be an onslaught of responses to the questions posed for weeks to come.

Having done the lion's share of work in the preparation for painting the mural—Marta had used the schematic grid over the smaller version in transferring the painting to scale on the college history quad walls—transferring the project seemed like a breeze. Things were moving along quicker than she'd expected. Most important, she was proud of the results so far. She stood back and smiled at the day's work. The mural looked great, if she did say so herself.

Getting back to painting, Marta called out the next color she needed, and almost immediately Desi handed up the paint to her with a clean brush.

"I don't know what I would have done without your fiancé coming to Leif's house when I was sick," Marta casually mentioned through the respirator mask while feathering dove-colored clouds on top of the cornflower-blue sky.

"He's the most caring man I've ever met."

Funny, Marta thought *she'd* already met the most caring man in all of Heartlandia. Leif.

"You're a lucky woman," she said rather than debate the matter. "When's your wedding?"

"We want to get married the Saturday after Christmas."

"How lovely!" It was quickly approaching Thanksgiving, so that was soon.

"I'd love for you to come."

Wow. Once Marta finished the project and left town, could she handle turning right around and coming back and seeing Leif again, by then her pregnancy overshadowing everything else? Or would it be smart to stay on with Leif that extra month? She forced her attention back to painting rather than think about the possibility. "Please send me an invitation, and if there's any way I can make it, I'll be here."

Maybe that could be her backup plan. Leave, let Leif realize what he'd be missing for a month, then come back and force him to admit he cared about her. After laying down the rules, she'd quickly lost track of the "no strings" part, falling deeper each day for him. But was it reciprocal? She had no clue. In all of their crazy lovemaking, he'd never once uttered anything about her staying on with him. Shouldn't she be glad, because wouldn't that make leaving Heartlandia easier?

"Good afternoon, ladies." Leif's familiar voice threw her out of the confused thoughts.

She turned, saw the world's most masculine man holding a... "Hey. What's that?"

He had a wicker basket in his hand and looked a little awkward. "Lunch. Want to join us, Desi?"

The wise young woman backed off. "Oh, thanks, but I've got class in an hour. I'll just grab something from the cafeteria first."

Marta noticed Leif didn't try to persuade Desi otherwise and liked that he wanted to keep her for himself. As Marta finished what she was working on, Leif put the basket down and talked to Desi.

"Lilly's going to interview me a little later. Should I be scared?"

Desi lifted her brows, her creamy light brown skin glowing in the sun and her chocolate-colored eyes looking playful. "You mean will she put you on the hot seat?"

"Well, since you put it that way, yes."

"Let's just say she has a knack for getting more information than you realize."

Marta sensed Leif needed backup, so she came up behind him and wrapped her arms around his waist. "I'll protect you, baby."

He leaned into her embrace and she automatically relaxed just being near him. He twisted and put his free arm around her shoulders. "Then, I know I'm in good hands."

In a flash, their conversation had shifted from the interview to the moments they'd spent making love just that morning. Come to think of it, her hands *had* worked wonders on him. Waking in the early-morning light, finding each other, they'd brightened the outlook of the day from their bodies touching and tangling together. No wonder she'd been in such a great mood and had accomplished so much already this morning.

Desi stood watching them for a few moments. A soft, knowing smile crossed her full lips. "I'm going to leave you two lovebirds to your lunch. Eric has signed up to help this afternoon. See you tomorrow, Marta."

"Thank you for organizing my crew," Marta said, realizing she already considered Desi a good friend. "I couldn't do this without you guys."

"No problem. Happy to do it. I'm learning so much."

Once Desi left, Leif kissed Marta soundly on the mouth, her open lips both an invitation and a promise for that night. He had that moony haze in his eyes she'd come to love whenever they ended their kisses, their ever-growing attraction buzzing between them. Who needed lunch? She did! She was pregnant and had an appetite like she'd never experienced before. It caused her stomach to growl at the mention of food.

He laughed at the condemning sound. "Good thing I stopped by."

They set up lunch on the grass under a nearby tree not far from the mural so they could keep an eye on it. Unfortunately, it was also not far enough away from the noisy campus and the between-class crowds, but it would have to do.

He'd brought carved-turkey sandwiches, obviously remembering her hesitation to eat deli meat while pregnant because of additives and the slim possibility of getting salmonella. She'd been devouring books on pregnancy each night, and to her surprise, Leif seemed as interested as she was in accumulating the knowledge. He'd also brought pears, apples and blackberries, a carton of milk for her and iced tea for himself. Ravenous from a good morning's work, she ate, thinking contented thoughts, sitting under the peekaboo sun with the man she adored and was constantly turned on by. Life was good.

Perhaps too good.

"You still gonna find me attractive when I'm fat?" she joked, taking a huge bite of sandwich and lightly punching his arm, then just as soon realizing she wouldn't be around when she was really big.

"I'm going to enjoy every minute of helping you get that way," he said with a gleam in his eyes as he handed her the carton of milk.

Oh, God, she could get used to this.

Was he talking about the whole pregnancy or just for while she was here? Did she want to spoil a lovely lunch with a great guy asking about a technicality?

She knew her home was in Sedona, and this was a job she'd been hired to do. It wasn't forever. Hadn't she been the one to lay down their rules for getting together—no strings, just for here and now? And that had seemed to be the final deciding factor for Leif. Everything they'd been enjoying together was icing on the cake, a lovely detour, but it couldn't be permanent.

She took another bite of her sandwich.

Could it?

Desi hadn't been kidding about Lilly. That afternoon, with minimal effort, the petite reporter managed to get Leif to open up about his mixed feelings on digging for treasure in sacred ground. He'd also explained his newly changed plans for going about the job with the intent of disturbing as little earth as possible.

Having pinpointed the one area of concentrated heat with the thermography studies, he planned to use an industrial fiber-optic scope to get a visual of the area. All he'd need to do was drill a three-inch-wide hole sixty to seventy feet deep, fit PVC piping inside for guidance and insert the lit fiber-optic scope to examine the area in question up close. Having made sure of the exact location of the suspected treasure trunk, they'd dig up as little area as necessary to remove it. Or, if there wasn't a buried trunk, they would only have disturbed a few inches diameter of soil—the depth, at the time of the interview, could only be approximated until he actually performed the task.

He realized even this procedure could be a bone of contention with those who opposed touching the burial ground in any way, but he also stressed it seemed the best compromise in this serious matter. And compromise was the bottom line.

Then Lilly dropped a bomb by asking if he'd heard about the Maritime Museum group expedition discovering what seemed to be parts of a sunken ship up the coast of the Columbia River. Speculation was it might possibly be the pirate ship mentioned in the captain's journals.

"Are you serious?" What else could happen in the cluster of baffling revelations?

Eyes big with excitement, she told him everything she knew.

The discovery had happened just that morning, and she'd been on site scribbling notes before coming to interview him. His first thought was, he couldn't wait to get home to tell Marta all about it. His second thought was, thank goodness, this might shift attention from the burial ground and divert some of the heat from his project.

"While I have you here…" Lilly said, her classic almond eyes offset by her borderline punk–style haircut. "I know Gunnar has thanked you, but I wanted you to know how much I love the add-on. Ever since I saw the blueprint, I knew it would be a special house, already was, but the addition, well, wow. Just wow."

Leif smiled—for a writer, she'd gone minimalist—then nodded, filled with satisfaction. "Gunnar knew exactly what he wanted."

"He did. And now that we're engaged, he's given me the okay to make a request."

"You mean I'm not done yet?" he teased, his interest piqued over what might be next.

"Nope." Though in her early thirties, Lilly still had the enthusiasm of a teenager. She handed him a picture of a small Japanese tea pavilion with a pagoda-style roof and wood pillars. It sat in a yard thick with woods, exactly like Gunnar's lot.

"This is beautiful," he said, excited about the chance to build something new and unique.

"I've got all kinds of plans for a teahouse, right on down to the shoji panels and Zen garden. You think you can build this for us? My parents and grandmother would be honored by it."

"Sure. I'd love to."

Lilly hugged Leif. He'd gotten out of practice in the hugging department, but thanks to Marta, he relaxed and enjoyed it. Even hugged back.

"One last thing," Lilly said. "Gunnar and I are having a get-together this Saturday night at Lincoln's Place to celebrate our engagement. We're inviting a few people, and since most of them will be Gunnar's friends, I'd love for you and Marta to come."

"That would be great," he said without hesitation. "Thanks for asking."

Well, how about that? First Marta brings me back from the dead, and now the town counts me in as one of the living.

It felt pretty damn good, too.

On Saturday night Marta emerged from her room looking nothing less than stunning. She'd pulled her hair back into a loose twist and wore extralarge gold double-hoop earrings. She divided a classic-cut white silk blouse and a full-length gold-textured satin skirt with a thick artisan leather belt. Gold Greek-style sandals spotlighted her bright red toenails.

Leif swallowed hard, fighting the impulse to sweep her up and take her straight to his bed. "You look gorgeous."

"Why, thank you. You look pretty damn great yourself."

He'd cleaned up wearing dark slacks and a pale violet dress shirt opened at the throat and with the cuffs rolled to his forearms. He'd even put on his black dress shoes, after searching way in the back of his old walk-in closet to find them.

Marta sauntered over to him and, careful not to mess her hair, he claimed her with a hand on the neck and a tug toward his mouth. They kissed long and tenderly, enough to jumble his brain cells. "You taste great, too," he said, regretfully ending the kiss.

Her caramel eyes looked dreamy and willing to do anything he asked. He loved that about her—knowing she wanted him as much as he wanted her. But she needed time with new friends and he wanted her to be happy. Breaking the moment, he glanced at his watch. "I guess we should go—"

"Or we might get in trouble?"

"You read my mind."

"It's a gift." She gave that saucy, confident expression that always got a rise out of him.

Cliff Lincoln had bought his restaurant after discovering Heartlandia while working as a chef on a cruise ship, and under his hand Lincoln's Place had become the local hot spot. A favorite tourist stop, the town was often overrun by cruise-line guests, pumping much-needed business into local commerce. Tonight, Gunnar and Lilly had taken over the bar area with their private party, though dining was still up and running in the adjacent restaurant.

"Hey, welcome, you guys." Lilly rushed to greet Leif and Marta with a glass of champagne in her hand.

Marta and Lilly hugged hello as Leif looked on smiling.

Lilly wore a cute fluffy-skirted cocktail dress in lavender, with a tight, shiny, sequined top and extra-high silver platform shoes, and she still only came to Gunnar's shoulder. Out of uniform, Gunnar looked rugged, like a younger version of Leif but with a whole lot more muscle mass. The man looked as if he could pull up a tree including the roots with his bare arms.

Heartlandia certainly knew how to grow gorgeous men.

"Help yourself to anything. It's an open bar," Gunnar said, already looking beyond to greet another couple. "Make yourselves at home," he added, moving off.

Leif asked the bartender for a draft beer for himself and club soda with a twist of lime for Marta. Drinks in hand, they roamed the room greeting folks; some were familiar faces and others she'd never seen before. They chatted and listened as someone told a joke that didn't really compute for her, but she laughed politely anyway. Her eyes wandered.

Elke, Gunnar's sister, sat at the end of the bar by herself, and Marta looked around for Ben because she always saw them together and had jumped to conclusions. He was nowhere in sight.

Marta slipped her hand out of Leif's and went over to say hello. "Where's Ben?"

Elke looked puzzled. "I'm not sure."

Feeling she'd put her foot in her mouth, Marta was about to apologize.

"He may stop by later, I think," Elke continued, a finger rubbing the rim of her wineglass.

"I see." Marta had assumed they were a couple since she'd first seen them at the town meetings. They often passed meaningful looks back and forth. At least that was how Marta had interpreted them—meaningful with something more simmering just beneath the surface. Longing? Plus, she could have sworn she'd seen them hold hands once on campus.

"We're not dating or anything, if that's what you're wondering."

Ah, another mind reader. Marta gave a playful grimace topped off with chagrin as she nodded. "I really sensed something between you. Excuse me."

A quick but definite wishful expression passed over Elke's features. "He's a great guy but doesn't socialize much."

Marta made note of Elke dressed very unlike her usual self in a little black dress, actually showing some shoulder and hinting at cleavage. "Too bad he'll miss seeing you like that. I think you look hot."

For a history professor who tended to imitate an old-school librarian in fashion, the change was refreshing, and Marta hoped Ben had the good sense to show up and get an eyeful.

Elke smiled and blushed.

From the corner of her vision, Marta saw an African-American man in a starched white chef shirt and pressed gray slacks, his cook's hat sitting at a jaunty angle. "Is that Cliff Lincoln?"

"Sure is," Elke said, turning her wineglass round and round by the stem. *That Ben better show up.*

Marta had learned all kinds of interesting tidbits about Cliff from her new friends Desi and Lilly. Like the fact that Cliff Lincoln, a Southern chef by nature, had started serving sushi after Lilly had kept hounding him about it. So tonight's table of appetizers not only included crawfish dip, fried green tomatoes, shrimp and grits and hot buffalo wings, but also California and rainbow rolls and assorted raw fish–style sushi bites.

"If you'll excuse me, I'm going to sample the goodies." Being pregnant, Marta avoided the raw fish but discovered something called a punk roll with a tempura-fried green bean at the core, and a hand roll made with a seaweed wrap, vegetables and rice. They were both divine. To her surprise, the fried green tomatoes complemented the other food on her plate.

The bar, filled with friends and a constant stream of cops, both off and on duty, was loud and congested. Marta hadn't been to a party since Lawrence had celebrated his last birthday, and though the atmosphere was more exclusive for that, the camaraderie and goodwill in Cliff's bar was far more enjoyable. But then, her mother's death had put every part of her relationship with Lawrence in a new light.

Thankful to have a smile put back on Marta's face, she noticed Ben Cobowa had managed to sneak in under the radar. As he headed right for Elke, Marta saw the young woman's face light up, and the sight warmed her heart. Maybe she was a mind reader after all.

Desi and Kent arrived a little late, both with a fresh flush to their faces, making Marta wonder what they'd been up to before they'd gotten here.

"Hi!" Desi called out, first hugging Lilly and Gunnar, then finding Marta. "You look gorgeous."

"Thanks. You're looking hot yourself."

Desi's tight red dress hugged her curves in all the right places, and from the admiring look in Kent's eyes, he'd probably been the one to pick it out.

"This little old thing?" Desi teased with an exaggerated Southern accent, then turned in a circle. "I only wear this when I don't care how I look." She'd quoted the sexy actress who'd played Violet from *It's a Wonderful Life* to a T, making Marta laugh.

Desi had told Marta while helping out at the mural that she'd grown up on the road with her mother playing piano bar in a Midwest hotel chain. Desi had also said she'd watched more than her share of old movies. Then they'd gotten into a contest over who could recite the most one-liners from all the classics. It had been a fun way to pass the afternoon painting, but Desi had won, hands down.

Leif wandered over and put his arm around Marta's

waist. Funny how great that simple gesture made her feel. As if she belonged to him. More and more lately, she *wanted* to belong to him, but she figured that was more than she could ask any man while being pregnant. Especially a proud someone like Leif, who'd once wanted his own family but had had the chance taken from him.

Desi's bright diamond engagement ring sparkled in the bar lights, catching Marta's eye. Was getting engaged the latest trend in Heartlandia? For an instant she let herself imagine how it might feel, then on an even greater whim, she pictured her mother's expression, if she were still alive, when Marta showed her an engagement ring of her own.

If you're looking down, Momma, I know how happy that would make you.

Cliff appeared at Desi's side, looking proud to host the engagement party. Desi had told Marta he'd been a mentor and father figure since she'd arrived in town— that he'd encouraged her to stay and even had given her a job. Some people actually thought they were related. They hugged hello.

Lilly rushed up to Cliff, popping some sushi into her mouth. "You did a great job on everything, especially the futomaki."

"What'd I tell you about cussing in public, young lady?" Cliff teased, pride spilling from his large black eyes in making one of the guests of honor happy.

The circle of friends laughed. Marta loved being a part of everything, especially being here as Leif's date.

"What this party needs is some music," Cliff said, shifting back to host mode and before Marta had the chance to go all melancholy. "Desi, you gonna play something?"

She shook her head. "I'm here as a guest tonight, and besides, you'd have to pay me more for private parties."

"Is that so?" He looked at Desi with a father's esteem, and Marta suddenly understood why Desi had asked him to walk her down the aisle in December.

In a few short moments, Latin music carried over the speakers and a handful of couples began to dance. It was a salsa and Marta loved to dance, so she moved her hips to the beat the slightest bit, making her skirt sway this way and that. In an instant, a familiar hand was at her back.

"Want to dance?" Leif said.

Completely surprised by the offer, never in her wildest dreams thinking of Leif as a dancer, she grinned. "Of course!" What could she be getting herself into? No matter how he performed, she'd pretend she loved to dance with him.

Expecting the worst but immediately pleased and dazzled by his smooth moves, Marta's grin stretched even wider. "How'd you learn the salsa?"

"Took some lessons. Sorry if I'm a little rusty."

"You did more than take lessons to dance like this. You're a natural."

"Not that natural. The Danes aren't exactly known for their dancing abilities."

She laughed softly, loving being with Leif, seeing him so much more relaxed than when she'd first met him. Moving with him. Thoroughly enjoying being out with friends in a new town, feeling the camaraderie and general goodwill from everyone. "So what's your secret?"

"Ellen made me take waltz lessons before we got married, and we enjoyed it so much we kept taking lessons.

It kind of became our thing. Worked our way through the Latin dances, and the rest, as they say, is history."

Though he smiled as he swayed his hips to the beat, she waited and watched for that distant look that always followed when he spoke of his wife. Tonight she either missed it or he hid it well. All she could see on his face was joy and sexy blue eyes gazing only at her, undressing her one item of clothing at a time.

Oh, God, this wasn't at all how it was supposed to be when she'd told him they could help heal each other. She'd meant it strictly clinically, not emotionally. He guided her hips outward to the beat and twirled her, then tugged her back to his chest. She draped her arms over his shoulders and, on a high from the fun dance, whispered into his ear. "Now I know why you're such a great lover."

He tilted his head back, eyes bright with a grin. "It's all about the hips, baby."

You got that right. And the passion that drives those hips.

The song ended and quickly morphed into a slow standard, and Leif pulled her close again. She knew, no matter how long she was back in Sedona, she'd never forget his musky leather scent and the strength of his arms whenever he held her. And all the potential she'd never get to see...

Naked. Tangled together. Leif still inside her. They snuggled after sex. Tonight had been particularly passionate. She thanked the hot Latin music they'd danced to all night. The best foreplay in the world.

Completely undone from the climax, she lay limp, breathing shallowly.

His hand came to rest on her stomach, where he rubbed lightly. He hadn't forgotten for a second that she was pregnant, that much she knew. Even if he tried to forget, her belly grew each day, reminding him. *This baby belongs to someone else.* She'd hardly been able to buckle her belt tonight. He kissed her forehead and withdrew, then made a quick visit to the bathroom. Behind the closed door, she heard him hum a happy tune. She'd brought life back into his existence, and he'd helped her forget the blow to her ego from Lawrence. *Lawrence who?*

And she was falling in love with Leif.

It was true. She couldn't deny it another second, even though it was the stupidest thing she'd ever done. Well, that, and wasting five years on a man who would never marry her. Why couldn't a girl listen to her mother?

Sunday evening Marta and Leif worked side by side in the kitchen. She'd prepared an apple crumble ready to go into the oven, and he dazzled her with whipping up a salad, then led her outside while he cooked cedar-plank salmon. He grilled it poolside on the designer barbecue. It was a chilly November evening and she wore her poncho to keep warm.

The dogs cavorted around the yard, eventually wandering over to test the scent from the grill.

"Sit," Leif said. Chip and Dale did as they were told. One yellow and one black Lab sat patiently side by side while he balanced a baby carrot on both of their snouts. "Stay." He stepped away. "Stay." Leif glanced at Marta and grinned; her heart flipped and pulse shimmied. "Staaay." He drew out the word.

Saliva hung in strands from both dogs' mouths, their patience weakening.

"Take it," Leif said, the dogs happily tossing the carrots into the air and, like magic, making them disappear.

Marta clapped with delight, laughing lightly. "You think they even tasted them?" The dogs rushed to her to check if she had a goody for them, too. All they got was a loving pat.

"Who knows, but they'd do that all day if I let them." A satisfied-looking man, Leif lifted the top on the grill to check the salmon. "Originally, when my buddy told me he had two Lab puppies left, I told him I'd take just one. I wanted the yellow dog. But when I went to get him, I saw the two of them rolling around playing, and I didn't have the heart to break them up. I decided they were a package deal and brought them both home. Smartest decision I ever made." He rubbed Chip's ears, then Dale's. "Wasn't it? Yeah."

So the guy had a heart for package deals. Might that give her hope for her own situation?

When the fish was done, he placed it in a dish covered in aluminum. They trekked back toward the house, where a salad and quinoa awaited. It was time to put the dessert into the oven, too. Approaching the kitchen door, she felt a pang of longing that was anything but subtle. It felt like home here. In five years, she'd never come close to this feeling with Lawrence, yet she'd settled for it, telling herself it was the life she wanted. More than likely because her mother kept telling her it wasn't.

She glanced at Leif, his warm smile smoothing over her feelings of loss and discontent as he held open the door, and with a steady gaze he watched as she walked inside. Chip and Dale pushed themselves between them and partially blocked the way, sniffing the air fragrant with cedar and salmon.

"Move it, guys." The dogs obeyed their master, hopefulness in their eyes about what might be in store for them for being good.

"You gonna want ice cream with dessert?" she asked, putting the dessert into the oven.

"Is there any other way to eat apple crumble?" He served a portion of salmon to each of the awaiting plates on the counter.

She opened the refrigerator. "What kind of salad dressing do you want?"

"I like that yogurt avocado stuff."

"Me, too."

Yeah, it felt like home—the kind her momma would have loved for her.

Later, they took a bath together. Leif was already in the tub and Marta slipped into the extrawarm water and settled between his legs. She leaned back against his solid chest, resting her head on his shoulder.

"This feels wonderful," she sighed.

His hands circled her in the sudsy water, finding her breasts and exploring. "You feel great." He nuzzled her neck, steam raising her temperature to match the vapor from the tub.

"Who would have guessed when you picked me up from the airport that we'd become lovers."

He let go a light laugh. "I thought you hated me."

"I didn't know you. I wasn't sure about staying at your house." *I was pregnant!*

His hands wandered to the insides of her thighs, then

up and over her belly and onward to lift her breasts again. She felt him harden behind her. "I'm really glad you did."

She sighed on an inhale as one hand found her folds and cupped her firmly. "It took a lot of convincing to get you here." She arched her back as his hand pressed tighter.

"I've been meaning to tell you how grateful I am." His hot breath over her ear added to the pleasure building inside. "But then, actions always speak louder than words."

"Do you want me?" she whispered.

"More and more each day." He didn't hesitate to answer.

Now his hand worked quickly, and her muscles tightened with the building anticipation and excitement.

"Aah." She sucked in air, soon rigid with need.

"Do *you* want *me*?"

"Yes. You." The word gasped from her lips as he brought her to release. "Only you."

He turned her to face him, and she straddled his lap as he proved again why she wanted and needed him. Only him.

Later, they lay wrapped together under the moonlight.

"You haven't said anything about my job tomorrow," he said.

He'd broached the topic she'd tabled since they realized they were on opposite sides. He was going to dig up sacred ground and she thought it was a horrible idea.

"You know how I feel about it. Nothing good can come from it."

"Okay. We won't rehash the situation. Why ruin a beautiful moment? I just want you to know I'm doing what the town voted to do."

"I understand."

Yeah, they'd drop the subject. Life wasn't always perfect, and this proved it. But in the dark, upset with what tomorrow would bring, Marta smiled toward the ceiling anyway. Remembering the beautifully simple and enlightening story about the dogs Leif had told while barbecuing, she rolled toward him and kissed his cheek. He'd proved with his Chip and Dale story to be a package-deal kind of guy. And why was she not surprised?

"You're an honorable man, Leif Andersen, and I respect that."

"Does that mean you understand about tomorrow?"

"Nope."

There were many more complications to their relationship beyond the great sex. But the biggest question remained—where to go from here? And, being a pregnant lady from out of town who'd talked him into having a just-for-now fling, that topic seemed nearly impossible to bring up.

He'd yet to come to her bed, his deceased wife still cutting a divide between them. She understood the significance, yet tonight they'd been together in the masterbath soaking tub. She'd take that as a step closer in the right direction.

The old, nagging thought of never being able to achieve what her parents had, that once-in-a lifetime love, kept her wondering in what "right" direction exactly did she want Leif to go. To be her prince, marry her, accept her baby as his? Dreams. All dreams. Foolish notions a mother had once tried to plant in a rebellious girl. Dreams she'd turned her back on all those years ago. Things she should never hope for now.

And yet...

Draped in Leif's embrace, Marta eventually slipped

from a fitful state into near sleep, with one last thought before conking out—if only he could see the package deal waiting in his arms.

Chapter Nine

Monday morning, bright and early, Leif left for the burial ground. The small work crew was meeting him there with the special equipment. Under the first light of day, a surprise awaited him.

"Did they camp out overnight? All weekend?" he muttered as he pulled his truck into the parking lot. No less than two dozen protestors waited at the Ringmuren. He recognized the lawyer from the meeting the other day—what was his name, William Maquinna? Plus several college-aged students he didn't know. Fortunately, Elke and Ben weren't among the group. It would have gotten really weird otherwise.

His guys waited in their trucks for him to take the lead. He didn't blame them—they were here to work, not to answer for their boss. May as well face it head-on.

Leif strode toward Mr. Maquinna. "Good morning,

sir. I understand your concern, and I want you to know that I plan to do as minimal disruption of this land as possible. I explained everything in the newspaper interview and I hope you've all read about my process." He glanced around at stoic faces; only Maquinna nodded.

"One teaspoon of earth is the same as digging up everything," said Mr. Maquinna.

"I hope you don't plan to disrupt the city-approved dig because, if I need to, I'll invite the police up here." Leif, speaking quiet yet firm, making his point as clear as possible, looked deep into the man's eyes, sizing him up. He understood Maquinna's sincerity in representing people long gone.

"And we hope our presence and the spirits of past generations will persuade you to stop." The lawyer stood his ground.

Point taken, but that wasn't going to happen. Nope. Leif needed to get this job done and put it in the past for the sake of everyone in Heartlandia.

After a few moments of silent standoff Maquinna spoke. "We mean you no harm, even though you are the one doing the damage."

Leif realized there was no appeasing the man or his group, and he had work to do, with expensive industrial equipment on loan and a mystery to solve for once and for always. But in his heart he hoped he wouldn't find a buried trunk since that would cause a much bigger excavation than he wanted or planned to do today, or, if he could help it, any other day.

"I don't see it that way, but we'll have to leave it at that." Leif considered offering his hand for a shake, but what if Maquinna didn't take it? The whole situation left a bad taste in his mouth, so he walked off.

Last night, in semisleeplessness he'd thought he'd devised a solution that could put the whole damn thing to rest.

Gravel popped and crunched on broken-down blacktop from tires behind him as another car drove into the parking lot. He turned, and his optimism for getting through this task without incident sunk to his gut. Ben, Elke and *Marta* got out of the car.

He and Marta had avoided this conversation like the apocalypse ever since the town meeting, distracting themselves with more pleasurable things. Like sex. They'd shared a few uneasy words last night but had quickly dropped the subject. Even now he hoped she'd come to support him.

He watched her. She studied him, and he thought he saw empathy in her expression, yet she followed Elke and Ben toward the group of protestors without uttering a word. Last night she'd seemed resigned about him doing this dig and in no uncertain terms made it known she didn't agree. He'd thought the topic had been settled. Hoped it had. They'd agreed to disagree. Now here she was supporting the opposite side, making him feel like crap. Her being here both stung and angered him.

He ground his teeth. *So that's how it was going to be.* Then he whistled to his team to bring the equipment. So much for loyalty. "Let's get this set up."

An eerie sound drew his attention as he continued on. William Maquinna had started to chant. Another man played a simple skin drum and another a wooden flute that looked and sounded like a recorder, sad and primitive. He kept walking, aware that gourd rattles mimicked his every step. Eerie.

He didn't believe in spirits and wasn't going to let

the group freak him out. Not right now anyway; he had business to take care of. Still, the hair on the back of his neck stood on end and he couldn't wait to wrap things up.

As he concentrated on the task at hand, what hurt most was knowing Marta was on the other side of the wall disapproving of his every move.

Well, so be it. He had a job to do.

Marta hadn't felt this queasy since her first trimester. Facing Leif had been gut-wrenching, his disappointment in seeing her obvious. But she had to stand up for what she believed in, even if it drove a wedge between her and the man she was falling in love with.

The similarities between her standoff with her mother popped into her mind. It had ruined their relationship. Did she want to risk that with Leif?

Lilly had arrived not long after she had and was snapping pictures and interviewing the protestors. Then she went around to the other side of the wall to talk to the crew, who promptly asked her to step back from the area. She took pictures anyway.

Marta inhaled a deep breath and removed herself from the group as the tribal music escalated to cries and squeals when Leif's crew made their first dig. The hydraulic device sounded like a giant dentist's drill and overpowered the protestors' wails. She knew Leif was using special equipment, something he called an earth auger, to contain the damage—she'd read the interview in the paper rather than bringing it up and risking another argument at home—and that he planned to dig straight down like they did for water wells. Then they'd check things out with the industrial fiber-optic scope before doing anything else.

The sound of the machinery was far worse than the actual hole they dug. Logically she understood he didn't want to damage the sacred ground, but the thought of disrespecting the land for potential profit didn't sit well with her sense of justice.

She spent the morning sketching faces, being there more as a spectator than a participant, but after a while the intense machinery noise and the high, whining chanting got to her. She needed to get away and remembered that special bench Leif had built for his mother. She walked the length of the park and outward to the shaded area in the woods and pine trees he'd taken her to the first time he'd brought her up here. A shard of light cut straight through the center of some trees and came to rest on the bench. She followed the light to the rugged wooden bench, made from natural planks with small tree branches for armrests and bench legs. The workmanship was distinct and familiar.

As she walked closer, she saw the words carved into the top plank on the backrest of the bench. "In loving memory of Hannah Anika Andersen, who loved her family and these beautiful trees. May her soul rest in peace."

Marta sat on the bench, which seemed to hug her. Leif had wished his mother's soul peace.

Her own mother's face came to mind, as clear as if she were standing right there. *I've got a secret to share, Momma. It took something you'd never approve of to figure it out, too. I'm going to be a mother, and, well, I hope you'll understand that I needed to take this path—the one you never approved of—to finally understand what you wanted for me. The baby has changed every aspect of my life. Turns out I want what you wanted for me all along. A good man. Love. Marriage. A family.*

But like you always said, when we go about things in the wrong way life gets more complicated than it should be. I hated when you told me that, thought all you wanted to do was hold me back, and my desire for independence drove me away from you. I was so determined to prove you and your traditional living wrong that I settled for things I never should have. I tricked myself into believing a modern, sophisticated relationship with Lawrence was everything I wanted, when in my heart I suspected it was only because he wouldn't offer more. I thought high living and jet-setting was good enough. Yet there was emptiness deep down, and I was too proud to admit it. You were right. Lawrence and I used each other. There, I've said it. Are you happy now?

I should have listened to you.

But if I had, my journey may never have brought me here...to meet Leif.

I think you'd like him, Momma. He even built this bench in honor of his mother.

And I never would have come here if I hadn't gotten pregnant. So you see...I wish you peace, just like Leif wishes his mother. I hope I find it, too.

The tribal music got louder, breaking into her thoughts. The carefully molded wood of the bench comforted her, yet desecration of sacred burial ground was occurring. She wiped the tears from the corners of her eyes from thinking about her mother and their unresolved, estranged relationship. Then her thoughts turned back to Leif and the reason she'd come here today.

She knew Leif understood the importance of letting those who have died before us rest. He'd probably go nuts if someone tried to cut down these trees or remove this bench; of course he wouldn't tear up the burial site unnec-essarily. She completely trusted his judgment. And him.

In the distance, the drilling stopped, and she assumed it was time to insert the PVC piping and then the indus-trial fiber-optic scope. She wanted to be near if Leif found anything, even though she dreaded it happening.

After paying respect to a woman she'd never met but one who'd raised a wonderful son and sending special loving thoughts to her own mother, she jogged back to the Ringmuren, wondering where in Heartlandia Ellen's bench was located.

Once back with the group, an announcement from Leif and his crew wasn't forthcoming, though everyone waited silently.

The protest group had thinned out as the morning had worn on and turned to afternoon. Ben was set to work the evening shift, and Elke had an afternoon class to teach, but Marta opted to stay on for Leif's sake. She needed to let him know she was more on his side than he thought. She honored his sense of duty to the city and understood his need for answers. She'd stay here all day if need be and wait for him to finish the job, then she'd ask him for a ride home—that was, if he wasn't furious with her. Again, having a strong sense of the man, she trusted he wouldn't be.

William Maquinna seemed almost in a trance from chanting and singing for so many hours. The drummer and flutist had stopped when the machinery had gone silent. The remaining group stood facing the wall, watch-ing and waiting. Practically holding their breath.

An hour later, Leif emerged from the other side of the Ringmuren covered in dirt, his expression completely impossible to read.

"Our expedition is complete. We've sealed up the three-inch hole we drilled today and replaced every last *spoonful* of dirt, and we will immediately be removing our equipment. Thank you for your patience. We've answered our question and will report our findings to the township committee. There won't be any need for further digging."

The Native American leader began to chant again and the drum, rattles and flute joined in with a lilting sacred melody. From what Marta could tell, the man seemed to be giving praise and asking forgiveness. The insult to the land hadn't been as bad as anyone had expected, and that was at least a small victory for everyone.

A little for this side, a little for the committee, no major harm nor foul, and best of all, the whole messy thing was over. Finally. Hopefully the spirits could forgive.

"I ask for healing of the earth and forgiveness from our ancestors," William Maquinna announced as the last of Leif's equipment was removed and his crew packed up and prepared to leave.

One last quick thought of her mother and whether she had forgiven Marta for stepping out of her life came to mind, followed by a swell of peace. Giving silent thanks, she looked to the treetops, then back at the small crowd.

Many of the gathered group stayed with Maquinna, but Marta set off to catch up to Leif.

So did Lilly. "What'd you find?"

"I have to report to the committee first, then we'll release the findings to the newspaper."

"I understand. Any thoughts?" She looked hopeful.

"I enjoyed the music all day." He gave a closed-lip,

noncommittal smile and Marta knew Lilly would have to back off for now.

Once he got to the truck, Leif turned, as if waiting, and watched cautiously as Marta peeled off from Lilly and approached him. With dirt on his face, dark smudges under his eyes and the dust turning his light hair brown, his blue eyes were more pronounced than ever. Without his saying a word, she understood he didn't hold a grudge about her being here today. She appreciated his tolerant attitude, wished she could be half as accepting of others as Leif was. He opened the cab door for her and she got in, their eyes meeting and melding an instant before he shut her in.

Minutes later, when they'd cleared the park and were halfway down the mountain Leif glanced at her, then back to the road. "It really crushed me to see you there today, you know."

"I'm sorry, but in my own way I was being supportive." She knew he wouldn't like seeing her there, yet she'd gone anyway, couldn't stay away.

"By standing with the other side?"

"Wouldn't I need a hard hat to be on your side?"

"Point taken."

"It's not as if I was chanting or anything."

"Now you're just grasping at straws."

"Sorry. I really didn't want to hurt you. Forgive me." The truth was, since her mother had died, he was the last person on Earth she ever wanted to hurt. "I know you're the kind of man who honors the tasks he gets assigned, even if things get tough. That when you feel committed to something, you see it through."

"That's right. When I start something I want to go all the way with it." He gave her a strange look, and she could have sworn she'd hit on something far more personal between them than a town protest. Now that she'd finally admitted what she wanted to her mother, would he be committed to seeing things through with her, too?

"That music got on my nerves," he said, watching the twists and turns of the winding road.

"And you're machinery got on their nerves."

He loosened up a bit, cracked a smile. "Good."

There wasn't any need to talk or argue anymore. The event was over, so they lapsed into silence again. It was reassuring to know that Leif was the kind of man who liked to finish what he started. Even though, theoretically, she'd been the one to start everything between them.

"I saw your mother's bench again today." She'd skip the part about talking to her own mother for now.

"You did?"

"Yeah, see, I didn't stay with the group the whole time. I sketched." She flipped through her pad as proof. "And I took a long walk. It's so beautiful. You did an incredible job."

"Thank you."

Her heart swelled with feelings and she wanted him to know some of them. "You're a loyal man. Your family must have been very proud of you."

"You didn't know me when I was a teenager."

"Same here. We probably would've hated each other."

"I find that hard to believe. On my end anyway." He dropped hint after hint about her, yet didn't bring up the subject she wanted most to have a conversation about—where they stood. Where did they stand? "Though you would have been way too young for me then."

"I was speaking theoretically. Anyway, if you hadn't

built the college and decided to have someone paint a mural—" *and if I'd never gotten pregnant* "—we would never have met."

"Pretty damn good decision on my part, wouldn't you say?"

She smiled and touched his arm; the sexual spark between them never faltered. "Outstanding."

After a quick shared smile, all seeming forgiven and glances promising more to come, things grew quiet again. It was clear he wasn't ready to talk about "them." Not now, after a taxing day dealing with ancient spirits and chanting protestors and new girlfriends standing with the wrong side.

But there was too much on Marta's mind to keep quiet, so it took all her strength to do so. She'd cut Leif a break for now and change the subject. She could push the man only so far.

She turned toward him, curiosity taking over her thoughts. "What did you find out?"

He chewed his lower lip in thought, then turned his head to her. "That no mystery trunk is worth disrupting a town or a cemetery over." Then immediately he looked back to the winding road.

"What do you mean?"

"I'm telling the committee when we meet tomorrow night that I found a dense deposit of bones, which I did." He stared straight ahead.

"And?"

"There may have been a trunk somewhere around there, too, but since I funded the study, I decided not to go blindly hunting for it, to leave things as they are in respect of the grounds. I won't mention that part—" he pinned her with flashing eyes "—and I hope you won't, either."

Subject closed. He didn't find a trunk, yet he hadn't really tried to find it once he'd discovered the bones. He trusted her with his secret. Now she knew more than ever he was an honorable man willing to do whatever was necessary for the greater good of his town. His study would be inconclusive for a pirate trunk.

He continued to drive, and Marta had yet another reason to love and admire the man. She turned her head and, looking out the window, smiled.

That night, while Leif showered and cleaned up, Marta made a simple meal of scrambled eggs with diced vegetables and cheese, toast and fruit, thinking how domestic she was and smiling the whole time. Leif had put an entirely new spin on the phrase *mi casa es su casa*. She felt completely at home here.

During dinner, choosing to talk about the family bench she'd visited instead of the elephant in the room— the digging at the burial ground—she got a phone call. Seeing who it was, she excused herself and went into the living room to take it. Leif watched her as Chip and Dale followed.

"Marta, it's Manny. How are you?"

Manuel Ortega was the Sedona historian and local quirky TV personality, his specialty being interview vignettes. The town joked and called him the Hispanic version of PBS's Huell Howser, one man with a cameraman and a hand microphone out to discover the state. Ask a question into the mic, then push it into the interviewee's face for an answer, over and over and over. Old school and loads of fun.

"I'm fine. What can I do for you?"

"I've heard about the mural you're painting for Heart-landia, and I want to bring a film crew to interview you."

"Wow, that's a surprise." She'd get to be the one under the spotlight?

"I thought it would be a great angle to be there for the finish. Is anything planned with the city? An unveiling?"

"Good question." She gave a nervous laugh, realizing she didn't have a clue if anything was planned or not. "I mean, I am almost finished, but I don't know about an unveiling or anything."

"Would next week be too soon to come?"

"No. I don't see why not. I've only got one last scene to paint and plan to start that tomorrow."

Leif hadn't *tried* to listen in to Marta's conversation, and it wasn't as though she was hiding anything from him, but she'd started pacing in the other room and one sentence stood out as she passed the large arch separating the living room from the dining room.

"I've only got one last scene to paint."

That certainly hit home. She was almost finished with the mural and would be returning to Sedona sooner than he'd expected. He fought back a spark of panic.

She'd laid down the rules for their relationship—no strings. Yet here he sat, all tangled up in strings since letting go and getting involved with her. Up until now he figured if she'd made the guidelines, she'd have to be the one to change them, but maybe it was time to confront her, see where they stood and if she was anywhere close to feeling the way he did. If so, it was time to come up with some new plans.

The thought of confronting her scared the living daylights out of him. What in the hell was he thinking? He shouldn't even consider changing anything until he was ready to admit he loved her. Did he love her? If he wasn't ready to admit he loved her, how would he be able to open his heart to her child? And even if he was ready to admit his love, would he be ready to be an automatic parent? Hell, could he even be a *good enough* parent for her baby?

Once upon a time, Ellen had believed he'd make a great father. Back then he'd believed it, too, but he was a lot older now.

Standing, he paced, too, his mind spinning with thoughts like plates on poles, but he disguised it by clearing the dishes from the table.

Calm down. He didn't even know if Marta had feelings anywhere near the same as him. She'd made the rules and, as far as he could tell, didn't have any plans to change them. At least she hadn't given him any indication in that regard.

Based on one single sentence indicating the project was almost done, his thoughts had launched out of control. He needed to get a grip, and more important, he needed to talk to someone who might know and understand how he was feeling.

One guy came to mind, a man who'd been through the ringer during and after his divorce. The good doctor, Kent Larson.

He removed his cell phone from his pocket and dialed Kent's number. Before Marta ended her call, he'd already made plans to have breakfast with Kent.

"You won't believe what just happened," she said, rushing into the kitchen to help dry the dishes he'd been washing like a madman. She didn't wait for his response.

"My hometown TV station is going to come and film me finishing the mural. This will be great promo for my art studio and store."

She looked flushed and excited, and Leif's heart sank a little because she also seemed to already have one foot, emotionally speaking, out the door.

Maybe he'd waited too long to tell her how he felt and had already blown it. "That's wonderful. When are they coming?" He fudged his way through his response, doing his best to appear excited for her good fortune. He didn't want to put a damper on her moment to shine.

"Next week."

"Great." Of course he was happy that she was getting some exposure in the media—he wanted her to be successful in her career—but it was the personal part, the going-back-home part—*the leaving-him-behind part*—that ached like a kick to the solar plexus.

The next morning at seven-thirty Leif met up with Kent at the Hartalanda Café in the center of town. Kent was dressed in slacks, shirt and tie for work at his medical clinic. They grabbed a table by the window and ordered coffee right off.

"What's up?" Kent got right to the point.

"I need some perspective and you seem like the right man to give it to me."

"Then I hope I can help."

The waitress brought mugs of hot coffee and took their orders, and Leif sampled the brew before laying his concerns on the line.

"So I've fallen for Marta." He shrugged off the mega confession. "It wasn't supposed to happen, but it did.

She's an incredible woman, and, well, I need some advice."

A lazy smile stretched across Kent's face. "Sounds as though it might be too late for advice."

Leif looked briefly at the ceiling, a sad, halfhearted laugh rolling out of his mouth. "Isn't that the truth?" He put his mug down and played with his fork. "How did you do it? I mean, after your wife left and you met Desi. How did you have the guts to just go for it again?"

It was Kent's turn to give the rueful laugh. "I didn't. Desi got that bright idea, and I resisted from the get-go."

"See, that's why I knew you'd understand."

"My advice is don't be a fool and drag your feet like I did. If you're thinking Marta is a woman you want to be with, go for it."

Leif felt a sheepish expression form on his face. "The thing is, I already have fallen for her, and I'm not sure she's in the same place I am. I mean, she's the first woman I've been with since Ellen, and maybe I got too wrapped up with her or something. Maybe I misunderstood her signals. How can you tell when a lady is into you?"

Kent sat back in his chair as the waitress brought their breakfasts with a benign smile. "Question of the century."

Leif didn't feel particularly hungry, but he made an unenthusiastic attempt to shovel in some pancakes and bacon. "Like I said, she's incredible, and I can't imagine...well, the way we are when we're together..." He put down his fork. "What I mean is, she can't be faking it. You know?"

Kent had his doctor face on. "You've got it bad. Have you told her?"

"Hell no. I've been out of the dating world for so long, I don't know how things work these days. Besides, she seems like such a modern woman, whatever that is."

"I'm not laughing at you," Kent said after smirking. "I know exactly how you feel. Felt the same way. The thing is, Desi was very persistent and, well, I'm a red-blooded guy, so..."

"Yeah, that's not the problem. It's the next part. The 'letting her know how I feel' part."

"Don't do what I did and come off all overbearing and completely unperceptive."

"So how did you find out if she loved you?"

"I tested the waters. Talked about how good we'd be as a couple. How much Steven adored her. That kind of thing. Eventually, she got the point and came around."

"Desi was going to leave town, too, wasn't she?"

"That's what I thought. Turns out she was just waiting for an invitation to stay."

Now, that made sense. Why should Marta stick around if she hadn't been invited and she had a place to go home to? How dense had Leif become during his hibernation?

Leif ate more of his pancakes, thinking about a way to first test the waters with Marta before laying it all out there. Their situation was different from Kent and Desi's because Marta was pregnant. *Wait! That's the test.* The father of her baby hadn't taken any interest. What if Leif told her his honest thoughts about her pregnancy? That he welcomed it. That he'd always wanted a big family. Maybe then he could win her trust and open the door to a long-term relationship. Or maybe he'd better start by just opening the door, see how she responded to that, then move on to the pregnancy.

"Thanks, man. You've helped me put some things into perspective."

"From the look on your face, you seem miserable." Kent had cleaned his plate and topped it off with a long draw from his mug of coffee. "Just let me say that opening up to love again isn't a death sentence. What I found out was it was a ticket back to life. Don't know what I'd do without Desi. Wait. Yes I do, I'd still be a shell. Lonely and miserable."

Leif nodded and took another drink of coffee. He could completely relate to being a shell of a man. It had been his MO ever since Ellen had died.

That night, Leif intended to make sure the committee meeting was short and sweet.

"Before we get started, I have a quick question," he said. "Are there any plans for an unveiling when the mural is finished?" Which it almost was. Even before he'd built the outer protection for the walls, he'd known she needed something better than ordinary ladders, so he'd loaned her a smaller-scale ladder scaffold, which essentially blocked out whichever part of the mural she worked on. Marta had told him she'd taken to leaving the finished portions of the walls behind the barrier he'd built, which hid the entire view, but he knew the mural was just about complete.

Elke spoke right up. "Yes. I've been working with the school administration and head of the art department. We plan a reveal for the college students first, then we'll open it up for a public walk-by. We're just waiting for Marta to give us a tentative date."

"Good. And I assume the newspaper will cover that."

"Oh, you bet. This is a first, and we're all thrilled with what we've seen so far."

For some crazy reason, hearing Elke's enthusiasm made pride well up inside Leif for Marta's accomplishments, even though theoretically he'd only played a small role by sponsoring the project.

"Okay, then, great. I guess we can get on with the purpose of the meeting." He glanced around the table at the six sets of eyes watching him and waiting for his report.

"Here are some of the pictures I snapped with the industrial fiber-optic scope." He took them from the folder and passed them around the table like show and tell. "The white areas are bones. Piles and piles of bones. Elke has examined the photographs and agrees that they prove this area was truly a burial ground. Evidently those bones are what we originally found with the thermography study." He produced a copy of the original map and another of the burial ground, then used a pencil to point to the area being discussed. "Nathaniel Prince's handmade map seemed to point to the same spot, right here, yet this is what we discovered. Now, we could explore other nearby areas, even though there wasn't any indication of anything else in this vicinity under thermography, but it would be a crapshoot and would probably be futile. Oh, and it would really tick off a lot of people, as we've already found out."

Leif knew he would be preaching to the choir for half of the group with his next comment, so he concentrated on the small business and Maritime Museum representatives on the committee. "At the risk of digging wider and deeper without strong evidence for finding anything based on the thermography report and upsetting almost half of the town, I move that we suspend further investigation."

Silence fell over the room, and a few pairs of eyes squinted and re-examined the round photographs as seen through a three-centimeter industrial, fiber-optic camera. After a few more minutes of passing around the results and quiet mutterings, Gerda Rask suggested the committee take another vote.

When he got home that night Marta wasn't there and the house felt cold and drab. He speed-dialed her cell phone.

"Hi!" she said.

"Hey, I was wondering if I should fix a late dinner."

"Actually, I'm with Lilly and Desi and we're in Astoria at their crafter's market. We already ate here."

"Okay." A pang of disappointment drew his attention. "Sounds good." Astoria was the next town over and was noted for the big weekly farmer and crafter market. "I guess I'll see you later, then."

"Most definitely."

Her enthusiastic response took the edge off his original reaction, and he ended the call with a smile.

Chip and Dale needed feeding and a walk, so he had things to keep him busy, but when he came back into the house and ate soup from a can and cheese toast, the empty house felt way too big. How the hell had he lived here by himself for so many years? Did he really want to ever do that again?

He went upstairs, and because the door to the studio was open and he missed Marta filling up his house with life and her freewheeling spirit, he walked inside. How would the room, overflowing with supplies and paint, feel after she left?

A trickle of anxiety worked its way up his spine. He didn't want to think about it. Not yet.

There was an easel facing the largest window and he walked around to see what she'd been painting, other than the mural. His jaw dropped. It was a half-finished portrait of him, smiling like he couldn't remember doing in years—only since Marta had come into his life had he started up again. Chip and Dale were sketched in the background, waiting their turn to be made immortal. A small photograph was tacked to the wood of the easel. It was him, on the day when he'd first taken her to the Ringmuren, the day he'd also shown her his mother's memorial bench.

Was this a going-away gift? Something to remember her by?

Leif loathed the sound of *remember* and *her* in the same sentence.

The soup he'd just eaten must have had too many tomatoes in it, because his stomach had suddenly turned sour.

If she left, he should at least be prepared with a parting gift of his own. But what?

A little after nine, Marta let herself in. Leif had on the evening news while he carved a small piece of teak wood. He quickly folded the towel over his lap and hid the figure he'd started under the chair, then clicked off the TV when she stepped into the room.

Looking happy and invigorated, she approached with a wide smile and some small bags. She bent and kissed him. He savored the kiss. Who knew how much longer he'd get them?

"How'd it go?" he asked.

"We had fun. Look." She wiggled the dangling bead and stone earrings from her lobes. "I got these and several pairs more from this supertalented jewelry maker."

"Nice. I like them."

She sat on his lap and ruffled through the bags, soon finding what else she'd hunted for. "I got this for you."

She handed him a necklace.

"Very nice. What is it?"

She cuffed his shoulder playfully. "It's a moon-mask necklace." She held it before his face by the thick leather strings so he could see it better. "It's made of abalone shell and carved wood."

As the pendant hung and shifted in the lamplight, he was taken by the changing colors and designs from the amazing seashell. It was enclosed by a delicate wood carving, with a funny moon face superimposed over the abalone, making the moon look as though it was ready to blow out a big wind onto the earth.

"That's really nice. Thank you. But you do realize I don't wear necklaces."

She undid the special leather knot and slipped the necklace over Leif's head. "You do now. When I saw this, I had to get it for you. It's made by a Chinook artist. He said the moon is a prophet with the desire to make the world a better place. I'm not saying you're a prophet or anything, but you make the world a better place. You build beautiful homes and colleges. Places where people can grow and be happy. So I said, 'Marta, you've got to buy this for Leif.'" She laughed insecurely, like a young girl, yet seeming so delighted with herself and the fanciful gift she'd given him.

"I like it." Her gesture touched a tender spot inside. "Thank you very much."

She rested her head on his shoulder and sighed. "I'm glad you like it."

They stayed quietly like that for a few moments, resting peacefully, and as his one hand skimmed her arm, Leif mindlessly fingered the handcrafted pendant with the other, wondering if this might be a second going-away gift from Marta. The portrait being the first, and this one, a predeparture gift. Now that he had a clear vision of what he wanted to make for her, plus a new project that just jumped to mind—a cradle—he'd better get moving on that carving so he'd have time to tackle the second.

With the insecure thoughts upending his peace, and because the right words hadn't come, he had a sudden need to take her to bed and make love to her, to prove how he felt about her. And as Kent had strongly advised him, there was no time like the present to get his point across.

Chapter Ten

Right there on the living room floor, on the rug in front of the fireplace—a rug he'd always thought of as useless until this perfect moment—Leif's desperate need to be inside Marta rushed things along. He stripped her and just as quickly undressed himself, leaving his new necklace in place so she'd notice.

With roaming hands reveling over the velvet softness of her skin, the feel of her breasts and abdomen, he used his mouth to make love to her. He opened her and made her ready for him. From all signs, she was as frantic for him as he was for her. Naked except for her new earrings, she looked like a seductive muse. His personal work of art.

He dazzled her with his tongue in all the best places, and when he settled between her legs, she dug into his hair, placing him just so.

He glanced up, and her silky olive-toned skin was slick with sheen. "You're so beautiful."

"So are you," she whispered.

Eager to please, he took her to the limit with his mouth, then, shifting upward, making eye contact before kissing her, he thrust inside, skydiving nearly straight off the cliff. First their bodies crashed together with need, but soon they found their rhythm and rode the flood of sensations on and on and on to the edge. Lingering there barely long enough to catch a breath, they fast-forwarded to whiteout bliss.

When he'd recovered, he lifted her from the thick and fuzzy area rug on the hardwood floor and carried her up the stairs to his bed.

Sweaty and spent from sex, they cuddled in bed under ribbons of full moonlight. Leif inhaled Marta's scent—sex, sweat and cinnamon spice—wondering when she left if he would ever forget her fragrance or the taste of her.

While they'd made love he'd noticed her baby bump had become more pronounced. Could the pregnancy grow that much from one week to the next? Was it crazy to wish the kid was his?

Now fascinated with the growth, his hand wandered to her belly and rubbed lightly. Remembering his conversation with Kent that morning, he thought maybe it was time to test the waters on their relationship.

"What are your plans after the mural's done?" His hand went still on her pregnant tummy.

She sighed. "I've got so much to catch up on back home. And no one knows I'm pregnant yet, so I suppose I'll have to deal with that. I should make a special trip to Phoenix to tell my father, too."

He went onto his elbow and looked square into her eyes. "Just so you know, if you want to stick around for a while, the door's always open here." There, he'd said it. And now he held his breath. The thought had occurred to him on several occasions, yet he hadn't had the nerve to approach the topic until Kent had told him he needed to. If he got a positive response, he'd mention the baby.

Her breath went still, a cautious look formed in her eyes. "Thank you," she said, locking the now questioning gaze onto his. "Sometimes I wish things could be different."

He searched her eyes, trying to figure out the meaning of *sometimes*.

"Sometimes? Like when you're being logical or realistic? Sometimes when you want to run away from it all, or sometimes when you think about sticking around Heartlandia?" *Or sometimes when you think you might be falling in love?* The way he'd meant it and the way he felt.

"All of the above."

He swallowed and pulled her close.

Maybe *sometimes* was a sign she was changing her mind, and that was all he could ask for now. In that case, patience was what he needed.

Yeah, too bad things weren't different, but... "They could be."

She pulled back from the hug, and from the corner of her eye she gave him an odd glance. "Could be? What could be?"

"Different. Things could be different."

"With the wave of a wand? Oh, I wish I believed in fairy tales."

Marta was an independent woman, unafraid to take on whatever life gave her. That was the impression she'd given him from the start. Under challenge in his personal life, Leif had withdrawn from the living; he'd curled into a ball and emotionally shut out the world...until Marta had forced him out. Marta, however, was a survivor. She didn't need him or anyone to make her complete.

Yet...sometimes. He held her tighter, wishing he could read her mind, still too unsure to say, "Why don't we give it a try?" How lame was that when *try* was the weakest word he knew? A person either did things or they didn't. The last thing she needed from him was a limp-wristed try. No. She deserved much better. "Is that how you see us, a fairy tale?"

"Strange woman shows up in town, pregnant, meets a prince of a guy...and they lived..." She flopped onto her pillow, back of hand to forehead. "Happily."

It had been her idea for them to get together—no strings. She'd made it very clear. And until he had more to offer than a good-hearted *try*, he'd have to honor that. "Sounds like a good story to me."

"As the saying goes—" she glanced wistfully at him "—we'll always have Heartlandia."

She's gone cynical. I already sound like a memory.

"And the door will always be open." His body ached for hers. How much longer would she be around to love? He reached out and found her, as heat and sparks and electricity arced over, around and through them, and he did the one thing they both perfectly understood—he made love to her again.

In the dark, after giving her body completely and unhesitatingly to Leif, Marta couldn't get her hopes up. Leif had taken a huge risk by inviting her to stick around. It blew her mind. And she'd played it down. True, what he'd said had been a major step in the right direction, but there was so much farther for him to go and their time together was running out. He'd taken her offer of "just for now" to heart, even offered to extend it. But she was giving up on those open-ended relationships now, and she'd promised her mother.

The baby had to come first from now on.

But hadn't Leif proved the other night, with his Chip and Dale story, to accept package deals?

If only he could see the package deal waiting in his arms.

Even though she'd been the one to lay down the rules, it would have to be up to him to change "just for now" into forever, the three of them. Because she couldn't and wouldn't set herself up for more heartbreak. Leif would have to be the one to reach out to her; this was his turf. He'd invited her to stay on, but what about the baby?

Each day she found herself more and more open to the possibility of staying with Leif. He'd been the one to suffer the most from love and losing. She had to consider that and respect his reluctance to love again. She might be pregnant, but he had the biggest risk to take by opening his heart. And his invitation was a huge step in the right direction.

Truth was, as bold a facade as she wore, she couldn't take a second rejection for her and the baby. It would break her spirit, and more now than ever, her baby would need a completely strong and capable mother if it was to be just the two of them. She'd be the sole provider, and that was why Manny's TV interview would be so important to her career away from Lawrence. Out on her own. Without a benefactor. Completely independent.

Hers and Leif's was a delicate situation. If she wasn't

pregnant, things could be different; they could be long-distance lovers, take things as they came. But she'd had a long talk with her mother. Maybe it was her turn to let her secret thoughts be known—that she was in love with him and expected more than "the door's open."

Why not tell him now?

"Leif?" she whispered.

Leif had drifted off to sleep. Deep sleep. She wasn't surprised after the vigorous effort he'd put into making love...twice. She smiled and lifted her head, then studied his face, having already memorized all the lines and angles. She painted his portrait from a photograph, but when her job was done, before she left Heartlandia, if he let her go, she wanted to be able to paint him perfectly again...from memory.

Manny Ortega made a big splash entry onto the college campus in his Sedona TV news van the Monday after Thanksgiving. The "La Cucaracha" horn honk nearly threw Marta from the scaffolding. She was putting some finishing touches on the panel depicting the town monument her grandfather had sculpted.

After her heart settled and she figured out who it was, she waved.

The van came to an abrupt stop and the short and wide Manny popped out from the passenger side. *"Buenos dias, muchacha. Que paso?"* His normally curly hair was cropped close to his head.

"Hi. How are you?" She cleaned her hands, took off her mask and climbed down from the ladder scaffold. They hugged like old friends, though they were only acquaintances back home. She hitched her thumb over her shoulder. "So what do you think?"

"Wow, this looks beautiful. You'll have to paint one for Sedona. I know the perfect spot."

"To be honest, I prefer painting on canvas, but this has been a great experience." She'd worn loose-fitting overalls in the hopes of playing down the pregnancy during the interview. Tongues would wag soon enough back home; she didn't need to rush the gossip along just yet.

"Don't say another word until we get set up. Save all your thoughts for our interview, okay?"

"Sure."

It took another half hour for Manny and the camera guy to prepare. In the meantime, Desi utilized the brawn of a couple of the college football players who'd volunteered to help slide back all of the barriers from the rest of the mural. Since the town-monument vandalism, she'd taken to leaving the rest of the mural covered, even when she worked on the newest panel.

"Wow, this is something, *mujer*." Manny stood, arms akimbo, gaping at all of her hard work, making her feel proud of the effort. "Let's pan out from right here," he said to his partner, using his thumbs and index fingers to make a frame and looking inside. Back to business, he spent a couple of minutes discussing the best shots and deciding where Marta should stand and what lighting was best. As they discussed the interview, Marta and Manny slipped easily into speaking Spanish, the language her grandmother had taught her, and once everything was settled, before she realized it the tape was rolling and she needed to switch back to English again.

Halfway through the interview a figure moved through the gathering group of curious onlookers. She recognized Leif immediately. She glanced at him and he gave a friendly wave. Unable to do more, she blinked and nodded while answering Manny's latest question.

"What's going to be your next project?" Manny asked, then moved the microphone toward her.

Having a baby?

"Well, a certain Sedona representative suggested I paint another mural for my own hometown." Trying her best to be personable for the interview, she teased.

Their interchange went on for several more minutes as he asked her to explain the meaning of each portion of the panel. Then he threw her a curveball.

"So what will you paint for Sedona?"

"Wow, I'll have to give it some thought. Is that a real offer?" She grinned.

"As a matter of fact it is. I've been given the go-ahead to tell you a secret donor has funded the town mural for Sedona. What do you think?"

"I can't believe it!" Her hands flew to her cheeks. "How exciting."

The camera moved in close, and from Manny's ear-to-ear grin, he couldn't have looked happier with her reaction. She'd faked it, though. The questions swirled in her head, and it took extra concentration to focus on the interview again. After a few more questions and answers the interview ended, and boy was she glad. Having never been through anything like this before, she was worn out and stressed. One thought in particular nagged at her.

Was Lawrence behind this new offer, still trying to keep her under his thumb? If so, she'd never consent. Knowing who funded the mural would have to be included in her contract.

Marta glanced up, searching for Leif in the group of onlookers.

But he was nowhere around.

They'd shared a wonderful Thanksgiving with Gerda, Desi, Kent and his son, Steven. But Leif hadn't again broached the subject of her staying on after the mural again or becoming part of her package-deal condition. She couldn't very well force the topic. It was a good thing she hadn't told him she loved him. Opening his life to a ready-made family would have to be completely up to him. Because he was an honorable guy, she didn't want to influence his thinking and have him do the right thing on her behalf, like accepting a package deal when all he really wanted was the lady.

She'd spent the entire Thanksgiving weekend painting the mural undisturbed by students, other than the ones who'd volunteered to help. Because Gunnar had had some time off from the police department, he and Leif had worked nonstop on Lilly's teahouse.

These were good times. Thriving times. Yet their relationship had seemed to come to a standstill. Great sex, sure. The door had been left open for extending that, but there'd been no talk about the real future.

"I'm staying at the Heritage Hotel," Manny said after they finished the interview. "Why don't you join me for dinner tonight?"

Marta knew Manny's wife of thirtysomething years from the artist guild and understood him to be a proud grandfather, so she knew this wasn't a come-on. He was simply asking her to dinner.

A part of her wanted to run it by Leif, which seemed absurd for an independent woman, but there it was. He'd sneaked into her life on yet another level. "That'd be fun. Thanks."

After Manny and his cameraman broke down their

equipment and left, Marta couldn't concentrate to paint anymore and the day was only half-over. When the students Desi had assigned showed up for their after-lunch detail, she asked them to help her put things away and cover the mural with Leif's barrier on wheels.

Who would fund a mural in Sedona? She hoped it wasn't Lawrence and prayed it wasn't Leif trying to get rid of her. She wasn't ready to go home to Sedona, to face the people who didn't even know she was pregnant yet. And the last person she wanted to ever see again was Lawrence.

After her talk with her mother, she couldn't very well leave Heartlandia without being straightforward and letting Leif know how she felt about him.

Filled with confusing thoughts, restless and anxious, she took a short walk to think things through. More firm than ever, the only way she'd consent to paint a mural in Sedona was if Lawrence had nothing to do with it.

She bought some juice at the student store, then noticed a sign with an arrow pointing toward the Memorial Rose Garden. It was on the main path, and having a hunch, she followed it. The path soon forked, one way toward the English department buildings, the other toward the hillside. It was an easy choice, because that was toward the rose garden.

The campus was built on rolling slopes with commons all around and a beautiful view of the Columbia River off in the distance. She sipped her juice, never getting tired of looking at that river. Wandering farther and farther from the buildings, still following the arrows, she got lost in her thoughts. What if Leif funded the Sedona project as an easy way to let her go? What would she do then? Soon overcome with amazing scents—fragrant roses—she dropped that line of insecure thinking and found herself at the secluded garden on the outermost portion of the college.

And there she saw it—a beautifully carved wooden bench. Unlike the other two across town, this one was ornate and girlie. It was also a swing hanging from a rustic and sturdy frame made entirely from tree branches.

The abundance of roses scented the air, almost burning her nostrils, or maybe it was the rush of emotion fizzing through her body on seeing the swing. Walking solemnly toward the bench, she sensed an almost sacred aura around it. This was Ellen's. Leif had built and put it here with every ounce of love he possessed. She stepped closer to read the fancy calligraphy carved on a plaque resting atop a varnished tree-stump pedestal. "In memory of Ellen Andersen, the love of my life. Never to be forgotten."

The words hit like a kick behind the knees. Marta needed to sit down but didn't dare sit on Ellen's bench. She rushed away, toward the granite water fountain, leaned over for a drink as her own tears spilled into the water, then found a standard metal bench to recover.

One specific early conversation with Leif came to mind.

"How come you've never—" She'd ventured to ask a question that hadn't mattered nearly as much then as it did now.

Somehow, he'd known exactly what she was asking. "Remarried?"

It had turned out she wasn't the only one who could read minds and cut people off midsentence. "Because I can't imagine ever replacing her. I don't see how anyone can ever measure up. No woman wants to settle for replacement status."

Marta finally hoped for the love of her life, the kind of love her parents shared, but Leif had already found and lost his. She was pregnant with another man's baby, yet she had the crazy notion that a man like Leif, as loyal and devoted as they came, could see her for what she was—a woman in love with him. Someone willing to venture into a new life together. With him. If he was open to it.

From the start Marta must have come off as a seductress to Leif, preaching free love without strings. She wouldn't deny it was about time the man lived again, and she took pride in being a part of his reawakening. But only looking for a distraction to ward off the sting of Lawrence's rejection at the time, she hadn't bargained on falling for Leif. Now the big question was, would he take a chance on loving her and the baby, or was he even capable of it?

She glanced over her shoulder at the magnificent swing, the huge reminder of what stood between her and Leif, then looked down at her stomach, the other growing reminder why the odds were stacked against them.

Leif drove and drove. He had to keep moving, to occupy his mind, or his thoughts would eat at him. Marta had been happy and charming during the interview. Full of life and hope. Hell, she already had a job lined up back home. Why in the world would a bright light of a woman like that want to tie herself down with a ghost like him?

She'd practically had to pry him out of his rut, but damn if dangling sex like a carrot hadn't finally done the trick. Was that all that it was to her? And there was nothing wrong with that if it was. He was the jerk who'd projected emotions into the mix. They'd had a great thing going, the two of them, but he'd slipped up, let something that was never supposed to happen again occur—he'd fallen in love. Keeping it quiet was a cop-out, and now he'd have to tell her and take the consequences because he had to know one way or the other how she felt about him before she left. But the biggest question of all was, did he have the nerve to love again when life was a gamble and no one, not even Marta with her mind-reading ways, could predict what the future held? Did he have the strength to deal with losing love again?

Why did he feel as if he'd just been punched?

He drove in circles around a small park, then on to the houseboat section of town as he made plans on how and when to tell her how he felt. He couldn't call himself a man if he didn't. By his calculations, because the big reveal was planned for Monday next week, she'd be out of here by early December. Which gave him exactly this weekend to make his move.

His cell phone rang. Only then did he realize he'd been driving around aimlessly for a couple of hours. The dogs hadn't even complained.

"Leif? It's Marta. Listen, Manny Ortega has asked me to join him for dinner tonight, so I wanted to give you a heads-up."

He did his best not to sound disappointed. After all, she was a freewheeling, independent woman who didn't need a sad sack of a guy dragging her down. "Hey, that sounds great. Have a good time."

Well, he could check off tonight.

Maybe he better wait until after the big mural reveal before he announced how he really felt about her. The last thing he wanted to do was compete with her painting. Or come off like a jealous, crazed lover. When Leif finally came clean with his feelings, he wanted Marta's undivided attention.

In the meantime he had the night to get busy with his carving for Marta—a chunk of teakwood that had mysteriously taken on a life of its own. Then he'd get to work on the crib. It was actually a good thing she wouldn't be home tonight because he had so much to do.

Hours later, Leif lay in bed unable to sleep. It was almost one and Marta hadn't come home yet. He trusted her when she'd explained that Manny was a friend from her hometown. But what bothered him was how obviously she missed home. Manny had asked her to dinner and she'd leaped at the chance.

He heard the front door open. The dogs stirred and lightly whined. "It's okay, guys." The three of them lay quiet and listened as steps came up the stairs.

Leif's heart stuttered with disappointment when he realized she'd gone on to her own room.

The next morning felt like going back to square one, day one. Leif met up with Marta in the kitchen, a tentative smile on her face.

"Good morning," she said, already dressed in her work overalls. "I'm going to have to spend the rest of the week working like a madwoman on all of the finishing touches to the mural."

"I'd offer to help, but I promised Lilly I'd work on her teahouse and get it done before her parents come to visit for New Year's."

"I understand."

He found a sponge and wiped up some crumbs on the counter. "Got home late last night."

She nodded. "We got carried away with gossip from back home." She poured cereal into a bowl, cut up a banana on top and added milk. "The crazy man wants to stay on and film the reveal and interview some of the locals." She spooned a bite and crunched. "Also, I asked Manny to help me put my shop for sale or lease since he has so many connections in Sedona. From now on I just want to concentrate on painting."

"When are you planning to leave?"

"My flight is a couple of days after the unveiling."

He poured coffee from a curiously quivering carafe. She'd already bought her ticket home, even though he'd invited her to stay on awhile. "So soon?"

She touched his back; he turned and found her unsure gaze concentrating on his eyes. "I have a lot to take care of back home. It's been building up ever since I've been here. I can't dump all the responsibilities on my assistants. And I need to see my own doctor—not that I don't appreciate Kent's doing the obstetrical care."

"I understand." At least he was *trying* to understand. There was that lousy word again. It really was useless because no way, with all the *trying* in the world, did he understand. Not by a long shot.

How had things morphed so abruptly into this awkward, giant step back to the beginning? He took her hand and gently rubbed the palm with his thumb. "I missed you last night."

Her eyes cast downward. "It was late. I didn't want to wake you."

Something had changed between them, and he was clueless. "You wouldn't have."

Her thick lashes lifted, and those mink-warm eyes gazed earnestly into his. "Come sleep in my bed tonight."

His thumb stopped circling the meat of her palm. Why the sudden test? He shut down. Went still. "Not sure I'm ready."

"Why not, Leif?"

His knee-jerk reaction was to say, "You know why," but he bit it back. A long silence stretched on as she searched his eyes for an honest answer. One he wasn't prepared to give. He ground his molars tightly together while the elephant sat smack in the middle of the room.

Ellen.

Marta deserved an answer.

"I guess I'm still not ready to go there." *To love and lose, to withstand gut-wrenching pain, emptiness so deep I can't breathe. Not knowing how to go on living.*

She canted her head as if his words hurt her ears. "I see."

Disappointment lingered in the kitchen like a stale coffee. She'd tested him. He'd failed. He wasn't prepared to make the leap. Would he ever get over the loss that came with love?

But they both had obligations and work to do. He couldn't deal with the major issue still keeping them apart in a two-minute conversation on the go in the kitchen, especially when Marta seemed to already have one foot back home in Sedona. Already half-gone.

"Will you be home tonight?" Like a fool in love, he still craved her company, but he let her remove her hand from his.

"I plan to be."

"I'll grill something for dinner."

"Okay."

Civil, and sad. They went about their day independent from each other.

That night Marta apologized to Leif over the phone. Manny had asked her to take him to Lincoln's restaurant, saying he wanted to experience the nightlife in Heartlandia. Desi had even agreed to play the piano, even though it wasn't the weekend. Manny planned to film the scene for his show, too.

The truth was, Marta had been asking Leif to take her there for weeks, especially after the engagement party. Leif had figured he had plenty of time to take Marta, and honestly, he liked keeping her all to himself. Turned out he was wrong about having all the time in the world, and his selfishness had come back to kick him in the teeth.

Marta didn't ask Leif to join them, and it cut deep.

"I won't be late," she said over the phone.

"Stay out as long as you want," he said, meaning to sound perfectly fine with her enjoying herself without him, but it didn't come out anywhere near the way he'd meant. The only positive point out of the situation that night was he got a lot of work done on the cradle.

After sleeping in her room the rest of the week, obviously knowing Leif wouldn't go there, on Sunday Marta asked him to help with the final stage of the mural.

Because it was a cloudy morning, he wore a sweatshirt and she a bulky fisherman's sweater she'd bought from a knitting store in town. They bought takeout coffee, one high octane, the other decaf, and croissants from the local bakery, though Leif didn't have much of an appetite. From the way Marta picked at her croissant, she didn't, either.

"Elke got the bright idea to hang a huge curtain over the mural and to rig up a way to draw it up for the reveal. We bought all of this inexpensive material yesterday, enough to cover every inch of the walls. I'll need you to take down the barrier for good."

"What about the risk of someone defacing the mural?"

"Elke has arranged for school security tonight."

"But what about in the future?"

"We agreed it's a painting meant to be shared with all, not kept locked away."

As if on cue, Elke and Ben arrived by car, apparently having the same idea as Leif and Marta from the looks of takeout coffee cups and a bag in their hands.

"Hi!" Elke said, excitement brightening her face.

As they greeted each other, several more people arrived to help with the day's project, padding the distance ever expanding between them.

For the next several hours Leif and Ben broke down the sliding wood barrier. Elke and Marta used the scaffolding and held panel after panel of the sky-blue shiny polyester material in place as a male student used an industrial-strength stapler to tack it to the wood trim.

Afterward, several students from the theater arts and set design classes stitched the panels together and rigged up a way to raise the curtain using triple-braided cord every five feet. Someone explained to Leif the technique they'd used was makeshift Roman shade, whatever that meant. Leif nodded and pretended he understood. The end result was a scalloped valance accentuating the beautiful mixture of colors in Marta's rich and masterful mural, and Leif was impressed with the resourceful students.

The group applauded at the first rehearsal, and Leif snapped a panoramic picture on his phone, making sure to include Marta standing on the sideline, a burst of pride sharpening her gorgeous smile. Then he walked over and waited his turn to hug her.

"This is so fantastic," he whispered over her ear, loving the way she felt, intensifying how much he'd missed holding her. She held tightly, too.

Because of the group gathered around, Leif only kissed Marta lightly, but her lips seemed to welcome his. At least it was something. They all ordered fast food for lunch as they worked on the finishing touches, and by the time they'd finished and arrived home, it was dark.

Marta was exhausted, excited and a nervous wreck about Monday.

After a light dinner, Leif brought her some herbal tea—her favorite stress-relief chamomile blend—and a couple of oatmeal cookies where she sat in the living room.

"Thank you," she said, glancing up from her laptop computer.

He kissed the top of her head instead of her mouth, which was where he wanted to kiss her. "Anything I can do?" He hoped she'd catch his double entendre.

"Are you good at writing speeches?"

Well, that had fallen flat. He laughed softly, ruefully. "No. But if you need help relaxing I've got a few ideas." Not above trying to make his point a second time, he went for the obvious.

With every cell in his body he wanted her, but for the past week she had given him no hint of a sign that she wanted him.

As expected, she didn't respond to his less-than-subtle suggestion about making love to ease her tension, but she continued to stare at the computer screen, typing, deleting, *tsk-tsking* and typing more. Loss sneaked into his life like an insidious vapor, sucking the air out of him one breath at a time.

He couldn't very well carve with her in the room, so he went to the garage and put the finishing touches on the cradle, sanded it and prepared to stain the wood the color of Marta's eyes—walnut. He racked his brain trying to figure out how he and Marta had gotten derailed. What had happened? Had he wanted too little? Had she wanted more?

He'd tested the waters, like Kent had suggested, letting her know the door was open for her to stay on. But he hadn't mentioned the baby and, damn it, he should have.

Days had gone by, they'd started sleeping in separate rooms and in a few more days she'd be gone.

He worked furiously on his project and got lost with his own style of art, then was surprisingly happy with the outcome. Next he wanted to get back to the hand sculpture, to start sanding if he hoped to complete and stain it before she left, but not tonight. It was late and he still had to walk the dogs. Tomorrow was a big day for Marta and he needed to be there with his full support.

After caring for the dogs, he went back into the house to find Marta had gone to her room for the night. Instinct told him to go in, climb in the bed with her and hold her all night, but the nagging sense of being shut out stamped down his true desire. She obviously considered that the safe zone. One big question came to mind: When had their "just for now" turned to "is this the end?"

Monday morning, Marta dressed in a long colorful skirt with a white blouse and loose beige jacket to disguise the pregnancy. She wore a pair of silver earrings she'd bought at the craft fair and, on a whim, decided to leave her hair down with an ivory-colored comb holding one side back.

When they met up in the kitchen, she saw that Leif had put on a tweed sport coat, white button-down shirt and a new pair of jeans. Her pulse fluttered, admiring how handsome he looked, how rugged. When she noticed he wore the moon-face necklace on the outside of his shirt, she kissed his cheek.

"You ready for this?" he asked. "Your big day."

"Not nearly enough."

"The mural is beautiful. It's perfect. What are you worried about?"

"Artist insecurity, I guess. We depend on what others think of our work. I have to make a living."

"Realistically all it takes is one person who believes in you."

One person with a lot of cash. The sincerity in his eyes touched her soul, but she had to stop him from saying one more word. He'd said the door was open to stay on, but she was through with benefactors with benefits. "Been there. Done that, Leif. All I got was pregnant." She couldn't open the door to dependence again. She needed to stand on her own two feet. To prove to herself she could do it before she could be worthy of a good man's love.

"About that..." he started.

As he spoke, she inadvertently glanced at her watch. She was running late. "What? I'm sorry, Leif. I wish we had more time to talk now, but we've really got to get going."

She saw his eyes go dark, then shut down. Realizing she was the cause of that look hurt like a knife to the heart, but the clock ticked on.

He quickly recovered and, gentleman that he was, opened the back door for her to step outside first. The dreary weather from yesterday had moved on, leaving a clear, sunny, late-autumn sky, though her outlook as far as Leif was concerned felt socked in with heavy gray clouds. He opened her door and helped her up into the truck cab, then walked around to the other side. Marta took out her laptop and brought up her speech, anything to get her mind off how badly their love affair had turned out. First she'd wanted more from him, now he wanted more of her. Which, because of time constraints, she couldn't give. Another lesson to be learned: no-strings affairs were bogus. They didn't exist. Someone always got hurt. What a lousy idea she'd had. *Yes, Momma, I get it. Remember?*

He started the car and they drove off toward the college.

Since discovering Ellen's bench, Marta understood that Leif had found his one true love early in life and he'd lost her. Maybe in his mind that could never happen again, and Marta couldn't compete with a dead woman. With a setup like that, she'd never come close to being first place in his heart—hadn't he warned her about that when she'd first come on to him?—and the realization had taken her aback. So she'd stayed away from Leif the past several nights.

The question was, could she settle for being a not-quite-good-enough replacement for a dead wife? The answer was no. Even her mother would have approved of that decision.

And she hadn't even touched on the ramifications of being pregnant with another man's baby and how that would affect any long-term relationship with Leif. Theirs was a far too complicated relationship to work out in the short time left.

Yet was she crazy to still hope for his love? Her parents' brand of love.

A tiny voice far, far in the back of her mind whispered yes, so no matter how much she wanted to do otherwise, she'd continue to sleep in her guest room, waiting for Leif to show a sign he'd worked through that barrier... until she left for good.

When they arrived at the college, Leif bussed her lips and smiled. "You're going to knock them dead."

God, the man was ripping out her heart with kindness. "Thank you." She wrapped her arms around his chest, and her clutching at his back was from loss, not nerves.

He held her close and lightly rubbed her back. "Relax, they're going to love you."

Will you love me, Leif? "Thanks." She let go, stood straight, fluffed her hair and smoothed her jacket. "How do I look?"

"Beautiful. As always." His tender smile nearly sent her flying to the sky.

"Thank you. I'll never be able to thank you enough."

She turned and started to walk toward the podium and thought she heard him mumble, "I can think of several ways."

A large crowd had gathered on the sprawling lawn near the history quad. The shiny blue curtain sparkled under the glare, and excitement for the big reveal was palpable. Her nerves ratcheted up another notch.

Gerda explained how things would work and offered her a chair. As she waited, her thoughts returned quickly to Leif.

Today, as she had every day since finding Ellen's

bench, she'd go on with her life, concentrating on what was best for her, her baby and her career. She pasted a smile on her face as her heart pounded and she watched the theater arts students lift the curtain from her mural with only a tiny glitch in the form of one uncooperative rope and panel. They fixed it amazingly fast and hoisted the curtain the rest of the way. The large crowd, including the mayor and the police and fire department chiefs, broke into applause, and she could have sworn she heard scattered gasps of delight. The gratification was bittersweet considering what she stood to lose with Leif.

After the extended applause died down, Mayor Rask introduced her.

Marta used the small portable computer to bring up her speech, though she knew it by heart.

"First off, please forgive me, I'm an artist, not a public speaker." She inhaled, attempting to quell her nerves.

"Earlier this year, when I heard about Heartlandia's quest to find a mural artist to tell your story, I didn't think I stood a chance. I mean, I tend to paint huge canvases, but I'd never painted a whole mural before. But since I was looking for a change in my life, I challenged myself and submitted my name anyway. As they say, no risk, no gain. When the committee found out my grandfather was the artist who sculpted your town monument, they took a closer look at me and my body of work.

"With the guidance of Professor Elke Norling, I've told your history through art. All I can say is, the experience has been life changing. True, we had a little hiccup when I first arrived almost three months ago and the news broke about your town first being discovered by a pirate..." She paused as she heard an uncomfortable titter ripple through the crowd, then continued, "But I incorporated that precipitating incident into my mural and quickly moved on."

She looked up and smiled, her eyes immediately finding and settling on Leif. He smiled encouragingly, though she thought she detected pain in his expression.

"As many of you may already know, this project would have been scrapped without the determination of one man, Leif Andersen. Without his wholehearted belief in the mural, and in me, as well as his financial support, we'd have no reason to celebrate today. Without him, we'd be staring at blank beige stucco walls. He is the visionary who built this college, who wanted art on the walls. I was just the lucky person to get to do the job. And to be honest, that was all it was to me when I first arrived, just a job. But through Leif, I discovered there was so much more here. I hadn't merely been hired—I'd been welcomed and adopted by the town, and he set out to prove it by opening his home to me and by introducing me to so many of you. He shared the best views with me. He introduced me to the sacred spots, the Ringmuren, the burial ground, his parents' memorial benches. Did you know that though several miles apart, there is a straight view from his mother's to his father's bench? I just discovered that with binoculars the other day. And in the Memorial Rose Garden right here on campus there is a touching and beautiful homage to his wife. These are the special memories I will take with me. He taught me to see your town through the love in his eyes. Through Leif, I've gained a new family, and now I've fallen for you, Heartlandia."

Watching for his reaction, she saw his head dip and his eyes cast downward. Maybe she'd taken it too far—she'd practically admitted she loved him—but she wanted the town to know what a great man he was, how much this campus meant to him, how he deserved their thanks and respect. And she wanted him to know she understood how much he loved his wife. That she finally understood that kind of love was irreplaceable.

"So I'd like to publicly thank you, Leif." Surprised by the rush of emotion, Marta said the words with a fluttery voice. She cleared her throat. "Thank you for your vision and for giving me the opportunity to open my heart to the wonderful people of Heartlandia. A part of me will always remain here." She gestured toward the mural to the right of her.

"Thank you! And thank you, Heartlandia."

Applause, cheers, even Manny's silly "La Cucaracha" van horn chimed in to the celebration. Marta was stunned by the acceptance. Gerda stepped back behind the podium and gave Marta a hug, told her the mural was beyond her greatest expectations, then posed with her as Lilly took a photograph for the newspaper. She'd promised Lilly an interview in the afternoon and also agreed to be around for the next two days as the mural was opened to the general public. And she would leave for home on Wednesday.

Elke had gotten the bright idea to make extralarge postcards for keepsakes and for the cruise ship and bus tourists who regularly visited Heartlandia. Elke had also suggested Marta autograph the first hundred to hand out as keepsakes of the event right after the unveiling. Manny headed straight for her with microphone in hand, no doubt ready with more questions.

There wouldn't be a moment to steal to be with Leif, to tell him she finally got it, that she loved him anyway. And if one day he felt ready to go all in again, she'd be waiting.

Chapter Eleven

After Marta's speech, when everyone swarmed her, Leif spotted Kent in the crowd on the college campus and made a beeline for him. "You got a minute?"

"Sure. What's up?"

"Everything has backfired. I need some serious help."

Kent looked around the busy campus. "Want to go to the rose garden to talk?"

That stopped Leif cold. The rose garden? The very place Marta had just let on she knew about. The place where he'd pledged his undying love and devotion to his wife until his own death.

May as well face it.

"Sure. Why not?" Why not walk straight into the fire…because if he wanted Marta for the rest of his life, he'd have to deal with what held him back once and for all. And it had to be quick because she was leaving on

Wednesday. What with everything going on today, it would be a wash. That gave him one day, Tuesday, to convince Marta to stay.

They entered the rose garden and sat on the opposite side because there was no way Leif could have this conversation sitting on Ellen's bench. In his heart, though, he knew she'd understand. Hell, she'd told him to move on in that dream, hadn't she?

Once he had Kent's undivided attention and Leif homed in on why he'd brought Kent here, he opened up.

"So I tested the waters with Marta, let her know I was open to her staying on with me as long as she wanted."

"You said that?"

"Well, not in so many words, but I'm pretty sure I got my point across."

"Did you bring up the baby? Are you open to that, too?"

"Uh, no, but wouldn't she know that?"

Kent smiled. "Good try. So now you have to say everything out loud. Don't leave any chance for doubt. Oh, and you have to prove it, too."

Listening to Kent, Leif realized he'd been pretty damn vague. He hadn't even brought up the baby. Oh, man, he hadn't been anywhere close to direct.

"How in the hell am I supposed to prove it?"

Kent had a perplexed look on his face, as if asking, "Seriously, dude, you don't know how to do that?"

"You have to tell her you love her and the baby and you want her to stay."

The words set off a cold burst right in the center of his chest. *Man up, Andersen. It's for the woman you want to spend the rest of your life with.* "That's easy for you to say."

"I'm not saying it's easy, but it's what you've got to do."

Leif understood. If he wanted to be a part of the living again, he had to be willing to take a big risk.

They shook hands, and after Kent left, Leif went to Ellen's swing and stood staring.

You know I love you and I'll never forget you, but I've been so lonely since you've been gone. I had a dream where you told me it was okay to move on, to live my life, and now I've found someone I want to be with. He glanced up at the trees, hands on his hips. *I never saw this day coming because I'm scared to death feeling this way.* He gingerly sat on the swing, inhaled the fragrant roses, thought of his deceased wife's sweet face. *You'll always be a part of me, babe. You turned me into a man, made me the grown-up I am. The thing is, I can't go on wishing you were still alive. I can't keep hiding behind that god-awful pain when I lost you as an excuse never to love again. Nothing is certain in life, but I think you'd be the first to kick my butt into gear, right? If I want to love again, I've got to risk the pain that comes with it. There's no getting around it. You taught me to be a man, and now I've got to act like one. No offense, but I'm done being a ghost. I know you'd want this for me, too.*

He sat quietly in the garden on his wife's memorial bench, letting the peace of the moment shower over him. *Remember how much we wanted children? Well, I've got a chance to be a ready-made father, and as scary as that seems, I want to take it. You think I'll be a good dad?* A light breeze whisked past his cheek. It felt like a kiss and gave him chills. Sitting still for several more minutes, pondering how his life had changed for the better since a certain artist had showed up in town, he decided to go after what he wanted most. Marta.

Leif went home, changed his clothes and threw a

change in his backpack, loaded up the dogs and everything he'd need to finish his carving and drove to his dad's favorite camping spot at Fogarty Creek State Park. He'd take tonight, a night when Marta was booked to the hilt with activities, to plan his action. There was no way he'd let her leave town without knowing he loved her and he wanted to be a part of her and her baby's lives.

It was almost nine when Marta finally made it back to Leif's place. A light was on in the kitchen, and a simple note lay on the counter. "Gone camping. See you tomorrow. Be here. Leif."

Her optimistic attitude deflated. With only a couple days left before she went home, he'd chosen to go camping. What kind of message was he sending? What about spending time with her?

She worried her lip and pushed her hair back. Did she mean anything to him? She'd made so many mistakes, being the one to withdraw first, then expecting him to notice and come after her. How infantile was that? She'd expected too much too soon from a man who'd lived like a recluse for three years. He'd come a long way in the short time they'd been together, yet she expected more because she'd had a change of heart where love was concerned. How could the guy possibly keep up?

She shouldn't have said that part about Ellen in her speech today; that had probably pissed him off royally. Plus, she'd dodged him for several nights, using Manny as an excuse, and she'd sent him back into hiding…and he'd gone camping. Man, she'd really blown it.

She dialed his cell phone but it went straight to voice mail. "Come home. Please" was all she said.

Upset and tired yet restless and, worst of all, resigned,

she went upstairs. Glancing around her room, she decided to occupy her time in the big empty house breaking down what little she wanted to take from the studio and packing up her bags. Tomorrow was going to be another big and busy day, and who knew when she'd find time to prepare for her trip home otherwise?

She missed Leif with every breath. With each item she packed, anxiety grew inside. She had to tell him she loved him before she left. No more dancing around the borders on that. He was the best man she'd ever met, and he deserved to know that.

For the next several hours, Marta cleared out her drawers and closet, working furiously to distract herself but doing a terrible job. Weepy and confused, she continued filling two of her three suitcases, even taking them downstairs and hefting them into the trunk of her rental car in readiness, assuming she'd be driving herself to the airport on Wednesday. All she had left was her overnight bag and the clothes she intended to wear tomorrow and on the day she left town. The closet and drawers were empty, and she tucked away what remained in the bathroom for easy access. For all intents and purposes, her room was clear. Then she crashed on the bed, lonely, craving Leif with every thought but, thanks to the pregnancy, exhausted and in great need of sleep.

Tuesday morning, Leif packed up bright and early and drove straight home without even eating breakfast. He'd thought everything through and made his plans; now he couldn't wait to see Marta, to tell her he loved her and he wanted her here with him for the rest of his life.

Sure, he'd understand if she needed to make a trip home to put things in order and settle any unfinished business. Hell, he was a modern-day man, so he'd even understand if she went back to paint a mural for Sedona... as long as her place of residence was with him.

When he pulled into his driveway it was noon, and her rental car was gone. Good. He wanted to clean up, shave, shower and set up a few things before he saw her.

An hour later, he'd transformed from grungy to best dinner-out clothes. And he didn't mind saying so himself that he smelled damn sexy, too. He set about fixing up the living room, getting some logs ready for starting a fire when she got home and putting the completed carving, now wrapped and tied with a bow, on the coffee table. The cradle would be a surprise once he got her attention with everything else. It waited with one big pink and blue bow in the entry closet. He even brought down what was left of the candles he'd lit the first night they'd made love. Oh, and chocolate. He needed to make a run to the sweet shop in town for the best and most delicious Swiss chocolate to give Marta. He'd offer her sparkling non-alcoholic cider instead of champagne, too, so he needed to buy that to prove she and the baby were foremost in his thoughts. Wouldn't his second gift to her prove that?

And after he'd told her he loved her, the best way to prove he'd made the final leap over his fear of loving her all the way was to make love to her on his old bed in his old room. The room she'd tried to lure him back to but he'd refused, proving how scared he still was. He'd finally figured it all out sleeping under the stars. And today he wouldn't let her shut him out. He'd evolved and was ready to face his fears, embrace her and the baby, and she needed to know it without a doubt.

He rushed to the linen closet to find the best and sexiest sheets he owned. He'd change the bed and maybe set a couple of candles in there, too, then surprise her when he took her to bed.

His ear-to-ear grin plummeted to his chin when he opened the master bedroom doors. The drawers were askew, closet empty—even her suitcases were gone.

She'd already gone.

Hell, he hadn't gotten to say goodbye. To tell her he loved her. He dropped to a knee, his breath kicked out of him. He glanced through suddenly blurred vision at the emptiness and groaned.

She hadn't so much as left a note.

But her flight was scheduled for tomorrow. He was supposed to take her to the airport, just like the day he'd picked her up. Where in the hell did she go?

She still had to be in town. And if she was still in Heartlandia, he'd find her.

Panic setting in, his pulse beating rapid-fire, Leif catapulted out of the room and took the stairs like an indoor twister. He broke outside, sprinting to his truck.

Turning the ignition, he wondered if he was doomed to be alone forever. His parents had died early, his wife far too young, so he'd gotten used to being alone. But not anymore! He threw the truck into gear, drove like a maniac and fishtailed out of his driveway. Life was too short to live alone. He didn't want another moment to go by without Marta.

Kent's logic had clicked last night in the camp as he slept in his old pup tent. The reward for letting go and loving again would be much greater than any potential loss. Yet here he was already at the "loss" part and hating every second. He didn't want to be an old lonely man. He wanted to live and love, have a family. He'd defeat the gnawing fear this time around.

His heart was opened wide and there was more than enough room for both Marta and the baby. If she'd only have him. That was supposed to be his job today, to convince her beyond all doubt that they belonged together. All three of them. Now all he had to do was find her.

First he'd call the car rental to see if she'd returned the car. He pulled over to make the call, fumbling his way through finding the number.

With a sigh of relief he hung up. The car hadn't yet been returned. She still had to be in town. His brain was all jumbled. He hadn't been thinking clearly. Idiot. He called her cell. It went directly to voice mail.

"It's Leif. I need to talk to you. Call me, okay?"

For the next hour he drove like a madman all over town, up and down the main streets, searching for her and the rental car. She wasn't at the college, either. He called Lilly's cell. It also went directly to voice mail.

"This is Leif. Do you know where Marta is? Call me."

He drove to the train station on a crazy whim, thinking she might be there. Yeah, his brain cells were shot through and through with panic and fear; his actions didn't make much sense, but it was better than sitting still, twiddling his thumbs doing nothing and losing her. There was no sign of Marta at the train station, either. He'd started grasping at anything, anyplace, driving in circles.

On the verge of giving up, of admitting defeat, he pulled out of the art-supply parking lot, thinking of heading up to the Ringmuren, and spotted a police car. Gunnar Norling was driving. He honked and sped to catch the police sergeant.

Gunnar noticed him and pulled over. Leif jumped out

of his truck and strode toward Gunnar's car, where the cop had already gotten out.

"Have you seen Marta? She's gone. Didn't leave a note, and I can't find her anywhere. Her cell's turned…"

"Lilly and Desi are hosting a baby shower for her."

He stopped in his tracks. "A baby shower?"

Gunnar grimaced. "You know she's pregnant, right?"

"Of course I do." Leif understood he looked like a madman, but he wasn't stupid.

"They're having it early since she'll be leaving tomorrow." Gunnar glanced at his watch. "Should be over by now, though."

He felt completely out of the loop, but what could he expect when he and Marta had essentially quit communicating the past few days? Then the news dawned on him. She hadn't left town! She was still in Heartlandia. He still had a chance.

Like he'd been given a second start and was reenergized because of it, Leif sprinted back to his crazily parked car. "Thanks, man!"

"Drive carefully." Gunnar laughed the words.

Leif peeled out, hitting the highway like a race-car driver, figuring the most logical place to go was home.

Marta couldn't believe the sweet gesture her two new friends had made. They'd invited her to lunch, then surprised her with the baby shower. They'd also invited a handful of ladies from town, each someone Marta had quickly come to care about. Gerda Rask, Elke Norling, two art students she'd taken under her wing while painting the mural. Though Cliff Lincoln had offered his banquet room for the shower, he'd also stuck around and

became their private host for the afternoon, seeing to
their every need like a doting father.

Over coffee and cake, Desi filled her in on her true
love story with Kent. It occurred to Marta that when
love was right and meant to be, it was okay to trust and
depend on someone else. Necessary, even. Desi was
definitely a better woman for it and still remained independent and able to follow her dreams. It was time
to quit hiding behind that fear of a "benefactor" keeping her under his thumb. The only thing that mattered
was *who* the benefactor was and if he was the right man.
And Leif definitely was. When he'd asked her to stay on,
he knew she was a package deal. She and the baby had
both been invited.

Desi's story gave Marta hope she would find the same
balance and happiness for herself.

Hadn't she already without realizing it?

Desi followed Marta home to help carry in all of the
wonderful baby gifts she'd received and would have to
make arrangements to ship home. One more item to add
to her goodbye list. When they got there, a pang of dis-
appoint shot through Marta when she realized Leif's car
still wasn't home. Would he really stay AWOL on their
last day together?

There was so much she needed to tell him, to make
him understand. She loved him and wanted to be with
him…if he'd have her.

Heartsick that he would let her go without a proper
goodbye, she unlocked the front door and they went inside.

"Looks like someone's got some plans," Desi said
when they rushed by the living room and she noticed
the special setup.

Marta's hopes cautiously crawled out of the doldrums as she inspected the room. "I wonder what that is." She pointed to a box, definitely bigger than a ring box, with a huge bow.

"Let's get these boxes upstairs so I can clear out. I don't want to ruin any surprises, you know?" After Desi put the last package on the perfectly made bed, she hugged Marta.

They stared at the candles strategically placed around the room. Desi gave a mischievous smile and Marta got chill bumps on her arms. Leif had been in here, making plans.

"Maybe we better put the gifts over there." Desi pointed to the overstuffed lounger in the corner.

After they moved everything, Desi smoothed out the bedspread and winked. Then she left the room. "I want details, lady. Details!" She giggled as she went down the stairs, and a few seconds later Marta heard the door close tight.

What a great group of people her new friends were. Heartlandia felt more like home than Sedona, and the thought of leaving tomorrow made her chest ache. She glanced around her bedroom, which lifted her spirits. What was Leif up to?

To distract herself from her hopes getting too high, she went into the art studio and packed the unfinished portrait of Leif inside a large transport box. She planned to ship it home, finish it and bring it back to Leif in case he let her leave—another one of her last-ditch backup plans.

The back door slammed. "Marta! Marta!"

It was Leif, and he sounded desperate. Her pulse quivered and her breath got all screwy. "Up here." She could barely find the air to call out.

Rapid-fire feet pounded up the stairs. She opened the studio door, joy rushing into her veins. There he was, disheveled but really well dressed and wearing an urgent, earnest expression.

"Don't go. Stay with me. Please."

"Leif, I…"

"I love you."

He loves me? Her head went swimmy, and she tried to focus. "What about the baby? Wait. What? You love me?"

He stepped closer, took her hand, tugged her near. "I love every part of you, and that includes the baby." His eyes brightened, if that was even possible. "Wait. We've got to do this right. Come downstairs with me."

Pulling her along, he guided her downstairs to the living room. "Sit, sit." He put her in the plush wingback chair closest to the fireplace. Next he turned on the gas and lit the already assembled logs, then popped up and flipped a switch on the wall. Slow classical string music filtered through speakers hidden in the corners of the room.

"Oh, wait!" He rushed to the kitchen, opened the refrigerator door and came back with a bottle of chilled and sparkling apple cider. The glasses were already on the coffee table, but he didn't open the bottle or pour anything.

"I've made some gifts for you," he said, reaching for the pretty package with the maroon bow and handing it to her. He hovered over her as she opened it with shaky hands.

"Oh, Leif, this is beautiful. Did you carve it?"

He nodded. She turned the small sculpture this way and that, admiring the two figures melded together, one taller, the smaller one clearly pregnant with a baby outlined and etched inside the swell. She'd planned on being two against the world, but Leif's family idea felt far more appealing. She glanced up at him, tears blurring her vision. "Thank you."

"You're welcome, but wait, there's more." He dashed to the closet and pulled out the baby cradle.

Marta gasped. "Oh, my God, that's beautiful."

"I want both of you here with me."

Tears brimmed on her lids as he bent and hugged her. "When the baby's born, I'll carve his or her name right here."

"It's so beautiful. You've outdone yourself."

He dropped to one knee and took her hands in his.

"Please stay with me." The dogs had edged their way into the area, one butting him in the back, the other nudging her knee for a pat. "Stay with *us*. I love you. Make my life complete again."

She leaned into his arms, held him as if he'd disappear if she let go. "I love you, too." They kissed like the first time, fiery with passion and longing. God, she'd missed making out with him.

Then he stood and invited her to dance with him, and she joined him, gently swaying to the slow and quiet waltz.

"You deserve to hear the whole story," he said, one arm snug around her lower back, the other palm holding her hand. He kissed her fingers, then continued, "How you scared the hell out of me with your beauty and talent. I thought you were the most sophisticated woman on the planet and couldn't imagine you'd find anything about me appealing."

She couldn't resist kissing his cheek, then pressed hers next to his.

"But you kept chipping away at me." He spoke gently over her ear. "You came on so fast. How was I supposed to figure it all out? It was like some voodoo serum or something. I started feeling things. Dreaming about things. Wanting things. With you. I wanted you.

"And you were wise enough to already know that." He pulled back to look into her eyes. "Thank you."

"My pleasure."

"You tortured me, making it all sound so easy, so doable. Just for now. We can heal each other." He kissed her forehead. "You did heal me, Marta. Put feelings back into my heart. Thank you for not giving up."

Tears brimmed and threatened to spill over Marta's lids again. She had given up that very afternoon, and now he'd proved why she never, ever should have doubted him.

"That's why I want you to stay. Be with me. Let me be your home base. Let me give you and the baby a home. Let me love you from now until forever. I need you to tell me I can do that."

There was no doubt in Marta's mind that Leif knew how to love for eternity, that when he mated, he did it for life. That he was also a package-deal kind of guy, and he'd just offered everything to her. Well, almost everything. "Please do."

"Then, marry me." He said it with certainty, as though there was no doubt and she should make her decision right that instant.

Her breath got stuck in her windpipe; she was afraid to move, to jinx it, to lose this moment, but the guy needed and deserved an answer. She'd once put him on the spot and waited for him to act, and now things were the other way around.

She held his face with trembling fingers and looked deep into the blue depths of his eyes, the eyes of the man she loved with all of her strength and hope. "I was afraid you'd never ask me to stay, but I never dreamed of this. Yes. I want to marry you."

After another long and satisfying kiss, he took her hand and, forgetting about the cider and chocolate, walked her up the stairs and straight to her bedroom, then closed the door behind them.

Chapter Twelve

Two and a half years later...

It was a cloudy, blustery March day in Heartlandia.

"Gabriella needs a sweater," Marta called from the newly finished wraparound front porch—the two-year anniversary gift to her from the greatest husband in the world. From here, they could sit in the high-backed rocking chairs designed and handmade by Leif and watch sunsets and the Columbia River sparkle far off in the distance. They loved their sunsets together.

Leif played with their daughter as he loped in slow motion to catch her. The toddler giggled and ran away on the wide green lawn until she fell down.

"I got you!" Leif, acting like a huge monkey, chased after her, then swept her up from the ground.

"No! No!" Using her favorite word these days, Gabby halfheartedly fought her father.

"Mommy says you need a sweater, kitten. Aren't you cold?"

"Nooo!"

Leif pretended to eat her stomach, growling and laughing at the same time, then threw her over his shoulder like a bag of protesting potatoes.

"No, no, no, no."

Nothing meant more to Marta than to see Leif with her daughter. Their daughter. He'd married her before she'd delivered, giving Gabriella his last name and heart, sight unseen, and had never looked back. From the love and attention he gave, the child may as well have his blood running through her veins.

Leif made it to the porch railing, smiling up at her. "How're you feeling?"

"Fat," Marta said, rubbing her back and displaying her growing belly through the form-fitting top over leggings. "I just got a call from Kent."

"Everything okay?" He carefully put the sweater on Gabby, even though she squirmed like an octopus.

"Got the results of the amniocentesis back."

His eyes lit up. "And?"

"The baby's healthy."

"And?"

"I thought you didn't want to know the sex. Weren't you the one to turn your head during the ultrasound?"

"Maybe I lied."

"What kind of example is that for our daughter?"

He laughed. "Men are allowed to change their minds." Gabriella had settled down a little, as if knowing the importance of her parents talking about the new baby coming. He rushed up the steps and joined Marta there, tugging her near and kissing her. "I want to know. Especially if you do."

She decided to play it coy to draw out this wonderful moment. "I suppose it could be considered cruel and unusual punishment to expect me to keep a secret for four more months."

He kissed her again. "I'd hound you day and night. Tell me."

She put her hands together and pressed them to her lips, as if praying. "Okay. So remember those names we were tossing around last week?"

"Yes, now come on, you're driving me crazy." He tickled her sides, making her laugh. "How can I engrave the name on the cradle in time if you don't tell me?"

"You do have a point."

"Girl or boy?" He came at her with tickle fingers again.

She skipped aside to avoid more friendly torture. "It's a boy!"

He went still. "We're having a son?"

Delighted with the sudden over-the-moon expression on Leif's face, she laughed more. "That's generally what boy babies are called."

"Gabby, you're going to have a little brother! Isn't that fantastic?"

"Yay, fastic!" the child chimed in, clapping as if she'd just made a potty all by herself. "But I wanted a doggie." She pouted out her lower lip.

Leif looked at Marta with his usual she-says-the-cutest-things gaze, pride and love rolled together and welling in his eyes. Marta's vision blurred, taking in the two most important people in her life, one hand rubbing the ever-growing next addition to their family.

Her mother had a term for times like these. She called

them *golden moments*, and standing on the porch, gazing at her husband and daughter as they cheered for the coming baby, Marta decided this qualified for the greatest golden moment of her life.

That was, *after* that September day when she'd found and soon enough fell in love with Leif Andersen.

* * * * *

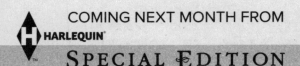

COMING NEXT MONTH FROM

HARLEQUIN®

SPECIAL EDITION

Available June 16, 2015

#2413 The Maverick's Accidental Bride
Montana Mavericks: What Happened at the Wedding?
by Christine Rimmer

Childhood pals Will Clifton and Jordyn Leigh Cates rekindle their friendship over punch at a summer wedding. That's the last thing they remember, and then they wake up married! As they puzzle out the circumstances of their nuptials, Will realizes that beautiful Jordyn—his *wife*—is all grown up. The rancher is determined to turn their "marriage" into reality and hold on to Jordyn's love...forever!

#2414 The Lawman Lassoes a Family
Conard County: The Next Generation • by Rachel Lee

Widow and single mother Vicki Templeton is new to Conard County, Wyoming. She's hoping for a second chance at life with her daughter. Little does she expect another shot at love, too, in the form of her next-door neighbor, Deputy Sheriff Dan Casey. He's also grieving the past, but Dan, Vicki and her little girl might just find their future as a family on the range.

#2415 The M.D.'s Unexpected Family
Rx for Love • by Cindy Kirk

Single dad Dr. Tim Duggan has his hands full with his twin daughters. The last thing he needs is a lovely woman distracting him from fatherhood and his job. But irrepressible Cassidy Kaye finds her way into his arms and his heart. After the hairstylist winds up pregnant, Tim's determined to make the bubbly beauty part of his family forever.

#2416 How to Marry a Doctor
Celebrations, Inc. • by Nancy Robards Thompson

Anna Adams knows her best friend, Dr. Jake Lennox, can't find a girlfriend to save his life. So she offers to set him up on five dates to find The One. Jake decides to find the perfect guy for Anna, as well...until he realizes that the only one he wants in Anna's arms is himself! Can the good doc diagnose a case of happily-ever-after—for himself and the alluring Anna?

#2417 Daddy Wore Spurs
Men of the West • by Stella Bagwell

When horse trainer Finn Calhoun learns he might be the father to a baby boy, he gallops off to Stallion Canyon, a ranch in northern California, to find out the truth. The infant's aunt and guardian, Mariah Montgomery, tries to resist the cowboy's charm, but this trio might just find the happiest ending in the West!

#2418 His Proposal, Their Forever
The Coles of Haley's Bay • by Melissa McClone

Artist Bailey Cole loves working at the local inn in Haley's Bay, Washington...but a very handsome, very dangerous threat looms. The hunky hotelier's name is Justin McMillian, and he's about to buy out Bailey's dreams from under her. As stubborn Bailey and sexy Justin butt heads over the project, then find common ground, sparks fly and kindle flames of true love.

YOU CAN FIND MORE INFORMATION ON UPCOMING HARLEQUIN® TITLES, FREE EXCERPTS AND MORE AT WWW.HARLEQUIN.COM.

HSECNM0615

REQUEST YOUR FREE BOOKS!

2 FREE NOVELS PLUS 2 FREE GIFTS!

◆ HARLEQUIN®

SPECIAL EDITION

Life, Love & Family

YES! Please send me 2 FREE Harlequin® Special Edition novels and my 2 FREE gifts (gifts are worth about $10). After receiving them, if I don't wish to receive any more books, I can return the shipping statement marked "cancel." If I don't cancel, I will receive 6 brand-new novels every month and be billed just $4.74 per book in the U.S. or $5.49 per book in Canada. That's a savings of at least 12% off the cover price! It's quite a bargain! Shipping and handling is just 50¢ per book in the U.S. and 75¢ per book in Canada.* I understand that accepting the 2 free books and gifts places me under no obligation to buy anything. I can always return a shipment and cancel at any time. Even if I never buy another book, the two free books and gifts are mine to keep forever.

235/335 HDN GH3Z

Name _____ (PLEASE PRINT) _____

Address _____ Apt. # _____

City _____ State/Prov. _____ Zip/Postal Code _____

Signature (if under 18, a parent or guardian must sign)

Mail to the **Reader Service:**
IN U.S.A.: P.O. Box 1867, Buffalo, NY 14240-1867
IN CANADA: P.O. Box 609, Fort Erie, Ontario L2A 5X3

Want to try two free books from another line?
Call 1-800-873-8635 or visit www.ReaderService.com.

* Terms and prices subject to change without notice. Prices do not include applicable taxes. Sales tax applicable in N.Y. Canadian residents will be charged applicable taxes. Offer not valid in Quebec. This offer is limited to one order per household. Not valid for current subscribers to Harlequin Special Edition books. All orders subject to credit approval. Credit or debit balances in a customer's account(s) may be offset by any other outstanding balance owed by or to the customer. Please allow 4 to 6 weeks for delivery. Offer available while quantities last.

Your Privacy—The Reader Service is committed to protecting your privacy. Our Privacy Policy is available online at www.ReaderService.com or upon request from the Reader Service.

We make a portion of our mailing list available to reputable third parties that offer products we believe may interest you. If you prefer that we not exchange your name with third parties, or if you wish to clarify or modify your communication preferences, please visit us at www.ReaderService.com/consumerchoice or write to us at Reader Service Preference Service, P.O. Box 9062, Buffalo, NY 14240-9062. Include your complete name and address.

HSE15

SPECIAL EXCERPT FROM

HARLEQUIN

SPECIAL EDITION

*New to Conard County, Wyoming, the last thing single mom
Vicki Templeton needs is a handsome distraction. But she
and her young daughter find so much more than a
next-door neighbor in Deputy Sheriff Dan Casey.
Is Dan the missing piece in their family portrait?*

Read on for a sneak preview of
THE LAWMAN LASSOES A FAMILY
by New York Times *bestselling author*
Rachel Lee,
the latest volume in the
CONARD COUNTY: THE NEXT GENERATION
miniseries.

Then, of course, there was Dan, who was still holding her
hand as if it were the most ordinary thing in the world. Once
again she noticed the warmth of his palm clasped to hers, the
strength of the fingers tangled with hers. Damn, something
about him called to her, but it could never be, simply because
he was a cop.

"I'm not making you feel smothered, am I?"

Startled, she looked at him. "No. How could you think
that? You've been helpful, but you haven't been hovering."

He laughed quietly. "Good. When you first arrived I had
two thoughts. You're Lena's niece, and I'm crazy about Lena,
so I wanted to make you feel at home. The second was…wait
for it…"

"Duty," she answered. "Caring for the cop's widow and kid."

She didn't know whether to laugh or cry. It was everywhere.

"Of course," he answered easily. "Nothing wrong with it. Even around here where the job is rarely dangerous, we all like knowing that we can depend on the others to keep an eye on our families. Nothing wrong with that. But I can see how it might go too far. And everyone's different, with different needs."

She sidestepped a little to avoid a place where the sidewalk was cracked and had heaved up. His hand seemed to steady her.

"Promise me something," he said.

"If I can."

"If I start to smother you, you'll tell me. I wouldn't want to do that."

"I'm not sure you could," she answered honestly. "But I promise."

He seemed to hesitate, very unlike him. "There was a third reason I wanted to help out," he said slowly.

"What was that?"

He surprised her. He stopped walking, and when she turned to face him, he took her gently by the shoulders. Before she understood what he was doing, he leaned in and kissed her lightly on the lips. Just a gentle kiss, the merest touching of their mouths, but she felt an electric shock run through her, felt something long quiescent spring to heated life.

Don't miss
THE LAWMAN LASSOES A FAMILY by Rachel Lee,
available July 2015 wherever
Harlequin® Special Edition books and ebooks are sold.

www.Harlequin.com